Alex Van Helsing

Voice of the Undead

Alex Van Helsing

Voice of the Undead

JASON HENDERSON

HarperTeen is an imprint of HarperCollins Publishers.

Alex Van Helsing: Voice of the Undead

www.epicreads.com

Library of Congress Cataloging-in-Publication Data
Henderson, Jason, 1971–
Voice of the undead / by Jason Henderson. — 1st ed.
p. cm. — (Alex Van Helsing)
Summary: After a fire damages his boarding school in Switzerland, fourteen-year-old Alex and his friends move to the girls' school across the lake, where supernatural happenings are disturbing the peace, and in the meantime, more Van Helsing family secrets are revealed.
ISBN 978-0-06-195101-5
[1. Horror stories. 2. Vampires—Fiction. 3. Supernatural—Fiction. 4. Boarding schools—Fiction. 5. Schools—Fiction. 6. Switzerland—Fiction.] I. Title.
PZ7.H37955Voi 2011 2010045554
[Fic]—dc22 CIP
AC

Typography by Joel Tippie
11 12 13 14 15 LP/RRDB 10 9 8 7 6 5 4 3 2 1
❖
First Edition

For Lorraine Bell, my grandmother

Chapter 1

Alex Van Helsing accelerated the gunmetal gray Kawasaki Ninja and watched the trees along the road around Lake Geneva melt into a twilight blur. Just a few miles to Glenarvon Academy, just a few more minutes, and no one would be the wiser.

Training had gone on longer than Alex had expected. What was supposed to be a late Saturday afternoon exercise with Sangster, his—what should he call Sangster?—*mentor*, had turned into a half-day ordeal. Sangster, who everyone else knew as Glenarvon's literature teacher, had let Alex join him and a team of active agents in a mock incursion into an enemy stronghold.

The "stronghold" was a small office building in

Secheron, the lakeside village where Alex and his friends sometimes went for ice cream; the exercise was a hyped-up version of Capture the Flag. Three agents were posing as terrorists holding a trio of "hostage" mannequins, and Alex joined the team that had to sneak in and neutralize the enemy without allowing the hostages to be harmed.

This was serious business to the agents of the Polidorium, a multinational organization, which a month before Alex had not known even existed. There were countless Polidorium agents scattered around the planet, but hundreds of them were located right here at their current Lake Geneva headquarters, and Sangster had been slowly allowing Alex access to that world. The exercise this morning had been a test of sorts. After a month of training one-on-one with Sangster, this was Alex's first time mixing with other agents.

Sid, Alex's gangly, excitable Canadian roommate at school, had been thrilled when he heard about the exercise. "It's like you're going to do a LARPG," Sid had said over Saturday morning breakfast in the Glenarvon dining hall. He had pronounced this acronym *larr-peg.*

"What is a LARPG?" Alex was already laughing. Sid's joy at a million things Alex had never heard of was infectious.

Sid put down his fork and gesticulated wildly with his hands. "That would be a live-action role-playing game."

"Have you ever done that?" Alex asked.

"Absolutely," Sid said. "In Montreal there's a yearly meeting of the NALAVRPG, that's the National Association of Live-Action Vampire-Role-Playing Games. I've been three times." Like Alex, Sid was fourteen, so going three times meant Sid had been doing this since he was—eleven? "I have a clan that—"

"Wait, wait, wait." Paul, Alex's other roommate, a beefy, British boy, nearly choked on his poached eggs. "*Stop.* That is the bloody saddest thing I have ever heard. How many people go to these things?"

"Thousands," said Sid. "They divide up into vampire hunters and fifteen classes of vampire. You've got your Nosferatu, your Tuxedos, your—"

Paul waved his arms. "Thousands of barmy people running around in costumes and stabbing one another with foam stakes. I think things that you have exposed me to are going to damage me forever."

"Anyway," said Alex. "We're gonna rescue some mannequins."

"You have the *coolest life,*" Sid said to Alex.

Paul looked around at the white plaster of the dining hall. Glenarvon was a converted castle, but the dining hall was the single drabbest feature of the place. "It must be nice, this having a life," he said wistfully. "Just don't miss curfew, mate. I can lie for you but Sid always turns pale, and the poor bloke can't get much paler."

Alex shrugged. "I won't miss curfew."

He was going to miss curfew. Alex and the commandos of the Polidorium had spent an hour and a half on the first mannequin-rescuing scenario, and then had switched sides, and then switched again. The last time around, Alex had attempted to sneak up on an enemy "vampire" but had been tagged: An agent playing a vampire heard him coming and marked him on the neck with a blotch of red ink—and decapitated the mannequins to boot. After that Alex had to play dead and lie there with the plaster people.

And then it was nine thirty. Alex realized he was going to be in trouble if he didn't make it back. Sangster had let him out early from the hour-long after-action review, and Alex was cut loose, finally on his own.

The road curved and then stretched out again for several miles, and Alex whipped around a couple of delivery trucks, upping his speed once he'd passed them.

He'd been nabbed missing curfew twice before. One more time and the RA would pass the paperwork up to

Headmaster Otranto, and there would be a talking-to and probably a call home to his parents. Alex couldn't have that.

You would think that Sangster would have been aware of this particular pressure. If he was, he was letting Alex manage it, as though learning to manage his schedule was part of his training. Fine.

He was hoping the ten P.M. curfew would be a little loose tonight—Sid and Paul were planning to join a bunch of the other guys in Aubrey House to watch a DVD in the lounge. With luck he could get back, ditch the motorcycle in the woods across from the main gate, and make it up to his room while the RAs started their rounds on the ground floor. Alex had to change, though; he was covered in ceiling plaster and gunpowder and had an enormous but washable red ink stain on his neck.

Alex felt a burst of static shoot through his brain, a whisper, and he darted his eyes left to catch the fleeting image of a figure in white disappearing behind a tree as he passed.

That was strange. As the bike roared down the road, picking up speed, Alex tapped a button on the side of his helmet and shouted into the microphone in front of his lips. "Sangster, are you there?"

No answer. Sangster must be out of pocket. But Alex knew what he had seen.

The feeling rose again. That feeling, that static behind his eyes, was the chief reason Sangster had taken him under his wing, even though he was only fourteen. The static burst and chopped in a wave through his mind and Alex saw another figure in white, blurring through the trees along the side of the road.

Alex slapped the button again. "Farmhouse, this is Van Helsing."

After a moment a voice came online. "Farmhouse."

In his mind, Alex could picture the farmhouse, so called because it was a small, unimpressive white house with a dilapidated metal garage door that sat in a clearing in the middle of the woods. The house was a ruse: The garage door opened to a tunnel that went a half mile underground, where the real farmhouse lived and breathed. It was a vast bunker of men and women and equipment, just one of many homes of the Polidorium.

"I'm seeing hostiles on the road from Secheron Village to Glenarvon Academy. Who is on point today?"

After a moment a female voice came on. "Alex, this is Armstrong, what's going on?"

Alex felt a moment's relief as he heard one of the few agents of the Polidorium he knew, or at least had interacted with more than once. "Something's up. I just saw two vampires by the side of the road, wearing Scholomance colors," Alex said, not turning back to look again. The Scholomance was a school, sort of; a school and a research facility and a massive organization all rolled into one. It lay below Lake Geneva behind mystical doors that were nearly impossible to find. And now two of its members were watching the road.

Alex headed toward the next big curve in the road, about a mile up. A pair of identical black Mercedes E-Class sedans came into view, rounding the curve, traveling his way in the opposing lane. His own lane clear, Alex sped up.

The second Mercedes drifted into the right lane, Alex's lane, to pass the first.

Alex eased off the throttle to give the vehicle time to get out of his lane. They were still half a mile away. He watched the passing Mercedes get up ahead of the other car, ready to move back into the opposing lane.

The Mercedes stayed in Alex's lane. Now they were side by side, two enormous black luxury sedans bearing down on him, blocking the road.

And then Alex felt it again, that hiss and static, rolling toward him like a cold wave.

In the dark of night Alex could not see even a hint of

the drivers, but he knew they would be white as bone, and strong and fanged. They intended to kill him.

Four hundred yards. Alex ran down the possibilities. *What's going on? They're blocking my path. Go into the woods?*

No. He needed to stick to the road. He needed to get back before the write-up and the call home.

The cars were about a yard and a half apart from each other. Alex sized up the space and throttled the Ninja again.

I've been made, he realized as he hurtled toward the cars. They were watching for *him*. Alex felt them speeding up as much as observed them.

Now he saw a vampire in white, tall, with black hair, step onto the shoulder, holding a device that at first he thought was a gun. But it wasn't a gun; it was long and rectangular, like a radio, and as the vampire stood still and Alex zipped past, he saw the vampire flip a switch.

"They've made me," Alex managed to say before he felt a burst of electricity shake through his helmet. He felt the pads of the helmet heat up and start to melt as the radio whined and sizzled inside.

Alex winced as the heat hit his ears and he had to reach up and yank the helmet off, letting it clatter on the road behind him.

The cars were still bearing down, and he was helmetless and alone.

At fifty yards he could see the clean black shine of the vehicles, and now he could finally glimpse the glistening white faces of the vampires within.

They were a race as old as his own, but made of sterner stuff; humans chosen and changed and tinged with the blood of ancient demons. They were fast and cunning. But Alex was no slouch. He aimed for the space between the vehicles.

Alex watched the cars' tires spinning, bearing down, and at ten yards he saw that the bone white faces inside could predict what he was going to do: try to cut between them. Which was why he wasn't going to do that. Alex waited until the left Mercedes's front wheel began to turn in, intending to mash him to jelly between the two cars. He broke and whipped left.

He heard the cars grind against each other with heavy brutality and steel as the Ninja sailed around the vehicles on the left. Alex dropped onto the gravel shoulder and then back on the road, throttling up.

Alex looked in the rearview mirror and saw them come around: With a fierce shriek of wheels against asphalt, the giant cars executed perfect opposite turns, swiveling back into separate lanes, traveling side by side once more. He heard the enormous German engines roar as they began to pursue him. By that time he was at least a mile ahead.

With his left hand Alex reached around into his Polidorium go package and drew out a long, slender weapon that was encased from end to end in black composite plastic. Called a Polibow, it fired bolts of silver and hawthorn wood, eight shots to a cartridge.

As he zoomed around the next curve, another car, small and French, came into view. He sailed past it, counting two people inside, civilians, and dismissed them. As he expected, the Mercedes wasted no time with them either, one of them tearing onto the shoulder to pass, the other passing on the left.

The road was clear. Alex watched the Mercedes in the mirror, gaining again. He needed to use his right hand for this. Alex passed the Polibow to his right hand and felt the bike immediately decelerate as he took his hand off the throttle and steered with the left. Alex turned his head, watching the cars instantly gain on him. He would get one shot and then they would be on him.

The road jolted and his arm swerved. He suppressed the urge to pull the trigger, breathed, and then fired. The bolt sailed out silently; only the small jolt in the Polibow let him know he had shot.

The passenger-side front wheel of the left Mercedes

exploded with a burst of white smoke and rubber. The car instantly turned right, slamming into the other Mercedes. For a moment the vampire behind the wheel of the right car held on, but then he lost it, spinning farther right and off the road.

Alex replaced the Polibow and gunned the throttle again as he watched the right Mercedes smash into a tree, a tiny exploding image in the rearview mirror. The left Mercedes, now missing a front tire, began to disappear into the distance behind him as he rounded another curve.

Suddenly Alex heard a new sound over his own engine, higher pitched, off to the right in the woods. A motorcycle.

Leaves and grass exploded on the side of the road as a candy-apple red Ducati 848, monstrous and fast, burst through the trees. Alex sped past and looked in the rearview. The Italian bike seemed to be driving itself.

Alex slapped a button on the side of the rearview, and the mirror instantly flipped over, showing an infrared image of the dark road. The creature on the bike wore leggings and the white robes of the Scholomance. The Ducati hit a bump and the pursuer's hood fell back.

The rider looked to be about sixteen or seventeen, her spiky yellow hair nearly flattened against her head. She smiled, thin lips coiling into a recognizable smirk that showed just a hint of fangs. *Elle.*

Alex drew the Polibow with his left hand, keeping his right on the throttle as the Ducati roared up beside him.

Elle rode alongside for a moment, watching him as they rocketed down the road.

"Where are you going?" she mouthed.

Alex looked into her blazing, dilated eyes and stuck there for a second. Suddenly he became aware of a shape in front of him, and he tore his eyes away to see a truck in the lane and had to hit the brakes and barrel around it. Elle mirrored him, coming around on the right and up alongside again.

"I'm a little busy," Alex shouted, raising the Polibow and aiming at Elle's chest. He breathed and fired, and the bolt sailed through the folds of her clothing.

Elle laughed silently. She twisted left and got up next to him, whipping out a long arm at his throat. Alex tried to move away and felt steely nails slash through his jacket.

He closed the gap again, coming side by side, the trees blurring behind her. The first time he had met her, Elle had nearly slaughtered his friends. Even among a psychotic race, she was crueler and wilder than most. He fired again, missing. Over her shoulder he saw a sign go by, GLENARVON, 1 KM.

Now Elle was reaching into her robe and drawing

something out. For a second he thought it was a weapon, dark and round. Then he saw it was moving.

Elle tossed whatever it was toward Alex. It landed on his arm—brownish red and potato-shaped, and then he realized it was something coiled, and uncoiling. Alex gasped as the potato unrolled into five small, slithering, wormlike creatures.

He got a look at them: red worms, about a hand's length, with tiny legs and black eyes, and spinning, churning teeth at the nose.

The worms began crawling over him and Alex swiped off one of them. Elle was laughing as another one latched on to his sleeve and burrowed in, its small body rising in the air as it twisted. He could feel the pressure of it as it bore down, like someone punching into his sleeve with a dowel rod.

What the hell are these?

Don't lose it. Breathe. One at a time.

Alex looked into Elle's eyes. She was enjoying his panic. So: *Don't panic. Let her enjoy it.* The worms were crawling on him and she was waiting to see if he would lose it or if one of them would get to his skin first. In that moment he raised the Polibow and shot.

The bolt caught Elle in the shoulder. She squealed, slamming sideways and tumbling off the bike, the red Ducati sailing end over end in Alex's rearview. He lost sight of Elle, but knew he had missed her heart. She'd be back.

One of the worms was at his neck and he grabbed it, pulling it away, feeling a pinch on the skin as it had already latched on. It squirmed in his glove, trying now to bite into his fingers, and he flicked it away.

The other one on his sleeve had made its way through, and Alex tried not to scream as he felt it make contact with his forearm.

What do you have?

Alex kept his right hand on the throttle even as the worm chewed and began to bite, and reached back with his left hand to find a glass ball. He brought the ball out, feeling its weight and the slosh of holy water inside. Alex smacked the ball on the front of the bike, cracking it like an egg, and brought it back, letting the water stream over his sleeve and body.

The worms hissed, their bodies bubbling and drying up. The one on his arm shriveled into a husk and Alex saw it blow away into the wind as he rounded one more turn and saw the main gate of Glenarvon Academy come into view.

Chapter 2

Within two minutes Alex had ditched the motorcycle in the woods across the road from the main gate of Glenarvon Academy and covered it over with leafy cut limbs. He switched to a regular bicycle, a more appropriate vehicle for a freshman heading into town, and pedaled through the gate. He was a little shocked to see his hands were shaky. The Scholomance had come for him. He had been genuinely surprised, and Alex Van Helsing was not used to being surprised.

No time for that now—he'd come this far and wasn't about to get busted yet. Dusty, jittery, and still ink-stained on the neck, he locked the bike at the rack and headed into the shadows of the hulking, forbidding castle that was Glenarvon's main house, Aubrey House, where he shared a room on the third floor. He hustled through the side entrance and bounded up the dim stairs, taking the steps two at a time.

As he came out the door into the third-floor hallway, Alex heard voices coming from the lounge and hesitated before moving past the door. He saw a room full of boys, all classes, gathered on couches and dragged-in extra chairs. Javi Arroyo, a senior and the RA for Aubrey House, had his back to the door as he fiddled with the DVD player next to the giant TV in the lounge.

"So I know everyone was hoping for *Doctor Zhivago*," Arroyo was saying as he plugged in an A/V wire, "but all we have is this thing about guys in metal suits." Arroyo turned around, holding up a copy of *Iron Man 2*. The crowd let it be known that they were duly appreciative not to be watching a three-hour movie about the Russian Revolution.

Alex hovered by the door until he saw Sid and Paul. Paul had commandeered a couch with Sid and had a giant bowl of popcorn. He was wearing a sweatsuit and sneakers, while Sid was still in his school uniform, his tie loosened. Alex remembered that Sid had been doing Academic Decathlon that afternoon. He caught their eyes and Sid made a gesture with open hands that somehow perfectly conveyed that Alex was cutting it a little close.

"Unfortunately it's dubbed in French," Javi said loudly, and the group groaned. Europe—you take what you can get.

Alex shrugged at his roommates and felt the jitteriness wearing off. He moved past the door and down the hall to his room. There, Alex threw his jacket and shirt on his bed and splashed at the sink in the tiny, white-plaster bathroom, scrubbing away at the ink on his neck. The room filled with steam from the hot water.

The vampires had tried to kill him. He'd lost his radio; he needed to call Sangster and do a debrief or an after-action or whatever the heck they would call it. He needed to talk.

A slight movement caught Alex's eye in the mirror, barely visible through the fog on the glass. Alex turned off the water and swiped at the condensation. He saw the silver gray of his jacket glinting in the dim light. Nothing. Satisfied with the now-nearly-invisible ink stain, he yanked a towel off the rack and patted his neck.

His jacket moved.

Alex turned, standing in the doorway of the bathroom, brushing his head against a baseball cap of Sid's that hung from the upper bunk next to the bathroom door. Across slick, tan-colored floor tiles strewn with the shoes, underwear, socks, wadded-up jeans, and sundry detritus of three fourteen-year-old boys stood Alex's bunk. And on it, his jacket sleeve was moving.

Worms.

Elle had thrown those things on him and he thought he had gotten them all, but now he realized one of the critters must have made it into his jacket somehow. He padded in bare feet across the room, grabbed a hockey stick from under the bookshelf next to the window, and turned to face the jacket.

Alex reached out with the hockey stick and touched the jacket sleeve. He saw it creep on the bed, wrinkling and bowing a bit. Alex put the stick against the collar of the jacket and dragged it onto the tiles.

The sleeve danced and wriggled. The bulb in the center where the creature lay began to move faster. Alex looked around to see if there was anything better he could use, past Sid's model kits and stacks of books. He could look through the go package, which lay on the floor.

No, that was ridiculous. He'd seen these things. They were worms. *Be a man, for Pete's sake.*

The sleeve danced again and Alex smacked it hard with the hockey stick. *Whunk.* The bulge in the jacket seemed to undulate and for a moment lay still. He whacked it again.

"That's more like it," Alex said.

The sleeve split and bloomed like a rose, cotton flying as the worm shot into the air. Alex was barely able to follow it as it zinged, spinning. It didn't look like a worm anymore: It was *growing*. The worm landed on Alex's headboard and grabbed on, because not only had it gotten bigger and split five or six ways, but it now had arms.

The creature appeared to be made of some dense, dark reddish material that reminded Alex of congealed blood. It was about eight inches tall, with claws for hands and claws for feet on four spindly limbs, and a face comprised of a single, swiveling set of teeth.

For a moment Alex stared at the blood-thing. Then it hissed, whipping its toothy head toward him, and he swiped hard at it with the stick. It leapt. The stick caught it at what Alex could only take for shoulders and it zinged through the air, landing on the door. Alex's stick followed through and took out a lamp his mom had sent him. The air filled with hundreds of multicolored glass shards.

The creature sprang with a whiny squeal and was on his chest, tiny claws crawling up his breastbone. Alex grabbed it, holding it out and away from him, and the tiny head whipped around and tried to chew at his thumbs. As it brushed its teeth against his hand, just missing his flesh, Alex saw the creature's back swell out like the throat of a frog in anticipation. It was ready to start sucking him dry. Alex gulped down his revulsion and threw the creature across the room.

The thing spun and slammed against Sid's bookshelf, sending plastic model airplane parts and brushes and tiny paint tubes flying. It dropped to the tile, limbs scrambling against the slick stone as it tried to find purchase. Running, Alex grabbed a handful of Sid's books and slammed them down on top of the creature. One hard lunge and he was sure he felt the thing squish under the stack.

Drops of sweat fell from his brow onto the copy of *Strange Creatures: Anthropology in Antiquity* under his hands.

No movement. Alex grabbed a couple more books, blinking against the smell of spilled turpentine, and stacked them on top of the rest.

Someone was pounding at the door. *Javi,* Alex thought.

Alex backed away from the bookshelf, watching for movement as the pounding grew louder. "Who is it?"

"Open up!" It was the voice of Bill Merrill, another

student. "Student" wasn't really an apt label. Bill Merrill was . . . a nightmare, a jerk, an old-fashioned bully. And he was rarely alone. *What could he possibly want?*

"I want our DS!" Bill shouted. He pounded again at the door.

Alex glanced around the room, taking his eyes off the stack of books. He called to the closed door, "Aren't those things against the rules?"

"Don't give me that," Bill retorted loudly, pounding the door again. "Open up."

Alex pulled on a T-shirt that said MY OTHER SHIRT BEARS AN ANTISOCIAL SENTIMENT and yanked the door open. "What?"

Bill Merrill, not as tall as Paul but bigger in every way than Alex, stood in the hallway. He was flanked by his silent brother, Steven. Bill did most of the talking, and most of it was hostile.

Bill pushed his way in and Steven followed. "We've been good to you, haven't we? We let you leave our room without a fuss," Bill said, shaking his head as he looked around. He was referring to the fact that Alex had originally been assigned to room with Bill and Steven, but they had made his life miserable until Alex moved out. This apparently qualified as a shared history. Bill touched some of the lamp's shattered glass with his shoes. "What are you doing in here?" He kicked at some random airplane parts.

"It's—"

"Never mind. Steven has a Nintendo DS that he thinks you took, and by you I don't mean you, I mean the person who does your fighting for you."

"You mean Minhi?" Alex asked, referring to Minhi Krishnaswami, a girl from LaLaurie School across the lake. Minhi was a kung fu expert and had beaten Bill once.

Mentioning Minhi made Steven, the silent brother, laugh. Bill frowned. "I mean *Paul*. Where did he put it?"

"Why would Paul want your DS?" A Nintendo DS—or any other gaming system—was strictly verboten at Glenarvon. But some students broke the rules, and the Merrills definitely fit that category. Alex couldn't think of a reason why his roommate would want to steal a game system from the Merrills, nor had he seen Paul playing on one.

"Maybe he just thinks it's funny," Bill said. He and Steven were idly searching the room, more with their eyes than anything.

Alex had had enough. "Look. I have to get changed."

Steven froze, staring up at the ceiling. Bill seemed to sense his brother's stopping and turned, looking up.

Alex saw it now, too. Neatly glued to a ceiling tile was a Nintendo DS.

Bill looked back at him, crossing his arms and blinking with something like innocence.

Alex said, "You have to admit, that *is* pretty funny . . ." but then he noticed that the books on the floor were starting to wobble the tiniest bit.

Steven looked at him silently and stepped up on the stack of books. He swiped up with one long arm, yanking the DS from of the ceiling. A puff of tile chalk ripped free as the DS came loose, and then Steven was falling.

Something was churning through the books and now *Strange Creatures: Anthropology in Antiquity* was dancing on end. It exploded in a burst of paper. The red worm creature, a starfish spinning in the air, soared and bounced off the wall. It landed on Steven's back as he found his footing.

"What the hell is that?" Bill yelled, momentarily shocked. Alex balled his fist into a towel and swiped at it across Steven's back, feeling it protest as it yanked free and flopped on the floor, spreading its starfishlike arms and breathing. "It's like a—what is that, a *bat*?"

Bill was already raising his dress shoe to stomp on it.

Yes, kill it, Alex thought. *Squish it before you get a good look at it.* Bill's foot came down and just caught it by the tail. The creature hissed and leapt, latching on to Bill's shoulder and springing out the open door.

Bill turned, seeing the red-brown creature clinging to a bulletin board filled with sheets of paper offering guitar lessons and begging rides into town from upperclassmen. Someone was putting together a rugby team and there was a sign-up sheet, with a pencil on a string.

With its upper arms spread and flattened, it did look vaguely batlike for a moment. Bill moved with a speed Alex would not have expected from him. He took less than a second to yank the pencil free and jam it through the creature, impaling it in corkboard.

Bill glanced back at his brother with an expression of satisfaction. Steven was coming out of the room with the DS, trying to see around his own shoulders.

"Come on. Are you all right?"

"I don't know, it *bit* me," Steven said again.

The brothers began to stomp back toward the lounge. Bill called back without looking, "I'm telling Otranto." Watching them go, Alex saw a slight trickle of blood on Steven's back.

Alex looked back at the impaled creature. He would need to clean it up. At least it hadn't—

It burst into flame.

Burst, just like a vampire, *fwoosh*, hot and fast, with

flames spattering out and catching all the paper and even the cork of the bulletin board instantly. Alex gasped.

Fire. *Put it out. Smother it.* His first thought was to yank the board down; the board was wide and flat and if he got it smack against the floor it would probably go out. He lost that plan in two seconds, because he yanked at the board and found it to be bolted in place.

Need a new plan. Alex turned, running into his room and grabbing his damp towel. He came back and tried patting at the board. But as it howled and crackled, Alex realized that already the cork had caught deep. Years of glue and ground-up corkboard where pushpins had entered and exited thousands of times had created a porous, well-oxygenated sheet of kindling. The towel had no effect other than to be singed by the flames.

Need a new plan. Fire extinguisher.

He started to run down the hall in the direction of the lounge, where students were watching the movie. He thought he heard Bill Merrill, angry about something. About ten or fifteen feet past the lounge was the stairwell where, he remembered, there was a fire extinguisher.

Alex passed a red fire-alarm handle on the wall. He grabbed it and yanked it down, and all at once alarms filled the air, heavy-sounding klaxons that split his ears.

Past the DVD watchers in the lounge. His mind registered that Steven was lying on the ground but only Bill had noticed, and everyone else was looking up at the sudden alarm sounds. Alex flew through the door into the stairwell, finding the lean yellow fire extinguisher and sliding it off its hooks. He booked it back down the hall, realizing he was running out of time.

PASS.

Pull-Aim-Squeeze-Sweep, he heard his father say in his mind.

Pull. As he ran, he yanked the metal safety pin that held the operating lever in place. Students were pouring into the hall behind him, shouting. Flames from the board had spread to the wallpaper and now were licking against the ceiling tiles.

Aim. He stopped and picked the base of the fire as his target, which in this case was still the board.

The flames began to spread across the ceiling tiles. Maybe they weren't past the tipping point yet, though. Maybe. *Squeeze.* He squeezed the handle up, waiting for the propellant to push back and up against his hands.

It did no such thing. Alex looked down at the markings on the extinguisher and read an expiration date that roughly coincided with one of his sister's births.

So there would be no *sweep* of the extinguisher's

contents because the propellant inside had dissipated years ago. Also, the ceiling was on fire.

Alex turned and ran, meeting Javi Arroyo next to the stairwell entrance, where he was shouting orders for everyone to move steadily down the stairs.

Bill was walking Steven with his arms under his shoulders. Steven looked pale. "What's wrong with him?" Alex called.

"I don't know," Bill said. Smoke was coming faster now.

A terrible thought occurred to Alex. "Is it because of the bite—" Alex said quickly.

"If it is, Van Helsing, I will *kill* you," Bill said, and disappeared down the stairwell, charging past several others, including Paul and Sid.

Great.

Alex looked back and saw flames licking across the ceiling, and starting to come out of his room.

"Alex, what are you doing?" Sid called.

The overhead lights began to flicker. Alex heard what must have been tubes of paint exploding in their room.

Javi slapped him on the back. "Come on, look alive," he said.

"There might be more we can do. . . ."

Javi shook his head. "The alarm is linked to the

village and the fire department can take it. Let's go."

Dismayed into silence, Alex joined Sid and Paul. Down the stairs the students moved as the alarms rang out, deafening them all.

Out at the gate, the whole school gathered and watched. Alex heard the RAs counting off students in the dark. Standing together, Alex, Paul, and Sid watched the upstairs, where the fire had moved from one room to at least two or three adjacent.

Alex heard Bill Merrill shouting and turned to look. A pair of teachers bent over Steven, who lay unconscious and deathly pale.

Paul tore his eyes away from the fire to nod toward Steven. "What happened to him?"

Elle. Elle. Freaking Elle.

"Something meant for me," Alex said.

There was a screeching of tires and Alex saw a racing green convertible scrape across gravel and stop near the gate. A man in his mid-thirties wearing a sport coat bounded out of the car. It was Sangster, with a look of horror. He saw Alex and relief crossed his face. The sounds of fire trucks filled the air.

Chapter 3

As alarms continued to flood the area with noise, paramedics burst through the crowd. Alex watched a young man in scrubs size up the situation instantly; almost no one needed help except for Steven, still prone.

Alex moved to Steven's side and found himself across from Bill, who looked up at him with disgust and worry.

"What happened to him?" the ambulance guy said in heavily accented English as he felt for a pulse. Steven's head was already elevated. He was unconscious but breathing. "Did he inhale smoke?"

"I don't think so," Bill said.

A woman in scrubs showed up with a gurney and the

two paramedics lifted Steven's body and laid it on the gurney.

"He was bitten," Alex volunteered.

The woman touched a metal lever next to the wheel base and the gurney popped up to waist height. "Bitten?" she asked, with the same French accent. "By what?"

"I don't know, it was a freakin' bat, I think," Bill said. "I've seen 'em in the rafters."

The paramedics nodded as they began to hurry with Steven. Bill ran with them.

The rest of the gate area was bedlam. Students were gathered in excitable groups. As the last of the fire trucks arrived and the ambulance sped away, Alex saw Headmaster Otranto talking intensely on a cell phone.

He was calling for buses. That was Otranto's skill: arranging things.

Even so, at eleven P.M. on a Friday this was not an easy task. They waited numbly for an hour until buses rolled in next to the fire trucks. The first order of business was loading the two hundred students of Glenarvon Academy onto the buses and getting them away from the academy itself, now soaked and smouldering.

From the back of his bus, Alex turned and watched out the glass window as the school gave off plumes of smoke. The entire upper story of the main house—where all the bedrooms were—was a wreck.

Alex realized that not listening to his own mind had done himself and his school a lot of damage. If he'd only noticed the worm in his jacket before he got back to the school . . . He had felt jittery when he got back and hadn't listened to the feeling. He had ruined everything.

The bus was full of chattering students borrowing one another's cell phones and calling America and Germany and Canada and the United Arab Emirates. Alex heard the phrase *going home* time and again.

Alex needed to call his own home, but he had left his cell in the saddlebags of his motorcycle in the trees across from the school, and the Polidorium Bluetooth was useful only for calling within and through the organization. After Paul had finished calling London, Alex borrowed his phone and called his family in Wyoming, where it was about four forty-five P.M.

His sister Ronnie answered. When she heard his voice, her first words were "Why are you calling from London?"

Alex scrunched back into the seat, looking at Paul. "What?"

"Your country code came in as London."

"I'm borrowing a cell phone."

"What's wrong?" she asked. Ronnie was twelve, Alex's closest friend in the world before he had left for one boarding school and then another. In the background he heard deafening music—classic rock, sounded like. She had to be in her room, tucked in the converted attic of a shambling Victorian monster that housed his parents and his four sisters. He could picture her, wavy black hair tucked into a wool cap, denim jacket. She was forever bundled up and guarded.

"It's a long story," Alex said, trying to sound serious but calm. "There's been an . . . are Mom and Dad home?"

"There's a thing at the university," Ronnie said. "Dad was actually wearing a bow tie. You can catch Mom on her cell if . . ."

There was a sharp *click* and he heard a second voice, also female. "Who's calling from London?" demanded Judith, who was fourteen and Alex's fraternal twin. The Sony cordless phones in the house had caller ID on every handset, so she was curious. That and she was nosy.

"NO ONE," Alex and Ronnie said immediately.

"Alex?" Judith snorted. "What did you do?"

"Why would you even say that?" Alex demanded.

"Because you usually call on Sundays and you're not using your own phone," Judith said evenly. She had her own soundtrack behind her, pulsating trip-hop and the persistent mechanical roar of a treadmill that was dwindling to a hum. She must be in the cavernous den of the house. Alex could picture her as well, probably in sleek Adidas sportswear, blond hair perfect and flowing, a picture of his mother.

Behind Judith, Alex could hear his little sisters, Frankie, who was ten, and Bobbi, who was eight, and the sounds of dishes being put down; this would be right off the den. "Is that Alex?" Bobbi shouted.

"You keep setting the table," Judith ordered.

"Judith would like to inform you that she is in charge," Ronnie said wryly.

"Which is why you're hiding out in your room?" Alex asked.

"What did you do?" Judith demanded again. "If Dad has to find another school to take you in . . ."

Ugh. She was just trying to goad him into fessing up to something, and there was nothing to fess up to. He chose to ignore the question. "There's no emergency right now," he said. "There's been an incident, a fire, so we're going somewhere else for the night. I don't know where. Just tell Mom and Dad I'll call when I get the chance."

"Have you been arrested?" Judith asked.

"Seriously, what is the matter with you?" Alex asked his twin. She had always been like this, a mental jujitsu artist, always pushing, then tugging, twisting, and trying to get you off balance.

"Whatever," Judith said. "I'll tell them you called. Ronnie, I know eating is important to you, so if you plan to join us I'll keep a place set for five minutes after the rest of us sit down."

"Don't you have a run to finish?" Ronnie asked. "Good-bye, Judith." After a moment they could hear Judith snort derisively and hang up.

Ronnie asked Alex, "Does all this have to do with the thing you haven't told Dad?" Alex winced at her straightforwardness. Ronnie never minced words.

What she meant was this: When Alex had arrived at Glenarvon Academy on Lake Geneva, he had learned a number of things he had not known before.

First, whereas Alex believed he had been going insane at Frayling Prep in the United States where he had gotten involved in a fight that left the other boy seriously injured, at Lake Geneva he had learned that he wasn't going crazy at all. Instead, he was beginning to be visited by a sense for evil, a static that grew and warned him of supernatural danger. The boy he'd fought had turned out to be particularly, supernaturally, dangerous.

Second, following the trail of this static had led Alex to discover that his father, a rather boring but renowned philanthropist and university lecturer on history and mythology, had fudged the truth during Alex's entire childhood. He had always insisted that the supernatural—vampires, zombies, the whole B-movie greatest-hits scene—were not real, were "not how things happened." Fudged as in lied. There *were* such things, and in Geneva, they had sought Alex out.

Third, his father should have *definitely* known better, because Dr. Van Helsing had actually been an agent for the organization that now called Alex one of its off-the-books fellows: the Polidorium. Apparently Dad had not known his old colleagues—and old enemies—were at Lake Geneva. But the memory of the vampires ran deep, and they had a special hatred—and a strange modicum of respect—for Alex's family.

Alex hadn't told his father about any of this. In the month since he'd made these discoveries, he had found a certain sense of belonging and peace in his new role. The Polidorium blanched at his youth but were training him because they seemed to believe his latent skill for finding and fighting the vampires could be a benefit to them, and therefore to their clients, which apparently extended to every government on the planet.

But he *had* told Ronnie.

"I think it's connected," Alex said now, and he looked around to make sure no one was listening. No one was—an evacuation after a fire had a way of putting everyone in an overexcited but unfocused state. As Alex ran his eyes up and down the bus—and out the window at the bus next to them—he saw dullness and confusion. He could have walked up and down the aisle stealing everyone's wallets and he doubted anyone would notice.

"People are going to know it started by my room," he said. Whispering, Alex gave Ronnie a brief run-down of the whole business of the evening. "I don't know what the school is going to do, but I'm gonna try to ride it out. I really need to stay."

"Ride it out?" Ronnie asked. "Okay. So you're going to tell Dad that you burned down your school, but assuming you don't get kicked out, 'don't worry about it because I like Switzerland so much'?"

He chuckled. "How did you so perfectly predict my line of argument?"

"We all live sprawled across one another," Ronnie grumbled. "Even in a house this big, even across the Atlantic." She seemed to consider the chessboard that lay before Alex. "It will work for now, but you have to cut them in soon."

"Why would you say that?"

"The best time to tell the truth is always soon," Ronnie said.

"Okay," Alex answered, looking out the window

again. "Anyway. We're off to—" Alex looked at Paul, who was talking to Sid, and raised his voice. "Where are we going?"

"Village Hall," Paul said.

Alex nodded and spoke to Ronnie. "Uh, Village Hall. In a place nearby called Secheron. I heard them saying we have to sit there while Otranto figures out where we can go for a few days. Or weeks. I don't know," he said again.

The only place that could hold them was the main room of the Secheron Village Hall, which would suffice for a few hours. The hall was big enough to hold two thousand citizens, with long rows of tables and metal chairs. The students filed in according to their houses and classes, and the administrators went about the business of keeping them occupied, with drinks and snacks being prepared in an industrial kitchen in the building.

While Otranto conferred with several of the other instructors, Sangster tapped Alex to go with him to pick up extra supplies from one of the few late-night grocery stores in town—an American-style superstore of the kind that was slowly infiltrating Europe. That errand was their way to escape and figure out what on earth was going on.

Into the woods the Glenarvon van shot with Sangster

at the wheel, heading toward Polidorium HQ. Alex was astonished that the instructor was able to find a path through the trees big enough for the van, but within ten minutes they were into the clearing he had come to know well, through the false door of the farmhouse, and down into the bowels of the earth.

Sangster brought the van to a stop in what amounted to a vast garage, big enough to house Humvees and cars and motorcycles and trucks with helicopters on their trailers. They bounded up the metal stairs at the back of the garage as Sangster gestured to a large clock on the wall. "We have an hour; that'll leave half an hour to get the supplies."

Through the doors at the top of the stairs lay a world of carpeting and glass walls. Alex heard the familiar clamor of agents moving from room to room, some listening to radio chatter, some drawing lines on enormous glass maps. Alex and Sangster moved past the commotion to a conference room, where two people waited impatiently.

At the head of a long, shiny black table sat Director Carreras, whose balding head and heavy-set frame fit his suit perfectly and made him look like the senior partner of a law firm. As they entered, Alex caught the eye of Agent Anne Armstrong, who was pacing near the projection screen at the front. She wore standard Polidorium togs, black pants and shirt, with shoulder holster. At least once in the month he'd been around, Alex had seen her in a U.S. Air Force uniform, and she had informed him she was actually a captain on detached assignment from that service. That was the way it worked, apparently. Some of these people were on loan.

"Can anyone tell me what is going on?" Sangster asked as Carreras bade them sit, and Armstrong's look indicated she had hoped to ask the same thing.

"We think it's retaliation against Van Helsing," said Carreras in a smooth British accent. "For the attack on the Scholomance last month."

For a moment Alex allowed it all to come back—the journey under the lake to reclaim his friends. But that adventure hadn't ended with a daring escape, the way he had expected it to when they managed to bash their way out alive.

No, the adventure had ended, truly ended, with Alex alone, a heavy vampiric hand wrapped around his throat. For a moment Alex saw again the flicker of red light, felt the nail of the vampire called Icemaker digging into him. Icemaker had been trying to raise a long-dead woman who would be the new queen of the vampires, and at that moment, with everything in his plan falling apart, she needed more blood. Alex was their last chance and he had almost died right there. The inch-long cut on his throat had only healed recently.

Alex shook the memory away and shared what had happened, from the Mercedes to the fire. Sangster said, "Tell us more about the worm."

Alex continued talking as Armstrong typed away. "It was about yea big," he said, holding out his hands. "It started out small and then it split into kind of a starfish."

"Did it have circular jaws?" Armstrong asked, not looking up. She tapped a key and on the screen appeared a three-dimensional diagram of the worm itself, slowly spinning, diagrammatic lines pointing to various parts of the creature.

"Yeah, that's it," Alex said.

"You ever seen one of these?" Armstrong said to Sangster.

"Only in Anzio," Sangster said, looking at the diagram.

"It's Italian?" Alex asked. Anzio was a coastal city where an enormous military cemetery stood. He had been there with his family.

"No, it's—Sangster is talking about the Polidorium's creature school in Anzio," Armstrong told him.

"Anyway: the worm is called a Glimmerhook. This is a very unusual thing for the Scholomance to haul out and throw at you. They would have had to procure it from one of the heavy-duty blood-wielding clans, the kind that can make enhanced creatures using blood. They come in an egglike, ah, grenade—so there are usually a handful of them, like you said. There're only one or two clan lords who can make them, so it would be an expensive get."

Alex remembered the worms crawling into his jacket. "What does it do?"

"Just two things," Armstrong said. "It sucks your blood and expands to carry back however much it can take, and oh, it poisons and kills you."

"Poisons? It bit one guy, Steven Merrill. He was in my room."

"Did you find him being bitten? How much blood—"

"I was there when it jumped on him and I pulled it off almost immediately," Alex answered. "Steven collapsed a few minutes later. He's in the hospital."

"How's he doing?" Armstrong asked.

"We won't know until tomorrow," Sangster said, shaking his head. "What will the effect of the worm look like?"

"Something like malaria," Armstrong said. "A blood

disease. It'll try to kill his white blood cells. It sounds like the bite was very brief. With any luck they'll treat him at the hospital and he'll pull through."

"You think so?" Alex asked.

Armstrong paused. "I guess I kind of hope so, Alex."

"So they hit him with an expensive and exotic weapon," Sangster said. "Doesn't that seem a little overboard for a retaliation?"

"What are you thinking?" Armstrong asked, searching Sangster's face. Alex watched her eyes dart; she had this way of scanning you like a map.

"I don't know. Tell me about the escalation you're seeing," Sangster replied. "It's a stretch, but maybe it's connected."

Armstrong turned her attention back to the keyboard and tapped some more. Information began to scroll down the wall, codes Alex could not read except that each was appended with a date and time down to the thousandth of a second. "When it comes to Scholomance activity, there absolutely has been an escalation," she said. "Just a week ago, Chatterbox looked pretty normal."

Alex raised a hand. "Chatterbox?"

Armstrong nodded. "This is something new we've been working on. It's still in its early stages—we have the main architect coming in to do some tweaks. Okay, actually, it's way beyond me, but it is very cool."

Now the screen began to arrange itself into a dynamic map of information—circles connected by dotted lines. As Armstrong swiped her hand, the map swiveled on its axis, showing more and more circles. She swiped her hand again and it stretched out chronologically; swiped again, and Alex saw topics laid out in idea groups *and* time.

"All of the information you see here," Armstrong said, "is compiled by computer, with human agents tweaking as they go. It's sweeping up emails, phone calls, texts, whatever we've managed to pick up. It's not easy because vampires tend to use phones and email addresses the way most criminals do—they keep them for a short time and toss them. Forums and chat rooms pop up and come down, and we at the Polidorium dedicate a lot of time to trolling all of these. Chatterbox looks for patterns."

As admirable as this was, Alex felt a little queasy. This was a scary tool.

Armstrong continued, "Anyway, Chatterbox as of last week was showing no particular focus for the Scholomance here. As of *yesterday* there was more chatter about Mira, which is their code for Lake Geneva."

"Why now?" he asked.

Armstrong tapped another key, and the line of communications grew into a map, with small red blips where different messages had appeared. As she trailed a finger over the tabletop, he saw each blip explode with information and keywords, *Mira*, *Polidorium*, and a plethora of other targeted phrases.

"Maybe they wanted you out of the way," Armstrong said, "because someone is coming to the Scholomance."

"Another clan lord?" Sangster asked.

Armstrong shook her head. "None of the clans have been chattering the way you'd expect if a lord was on the move—the way we knew Icemaker was coming. No, it's someone called by this other code word, *Ultravox*." She indicated the idea map, and swished her hand to now show ideas mapped in time and tagged geographically—circles moving up and down a map of Europe, building toward Switzerland. The keyword *Ultravox* glowed again and again.

"Who is Ultravox?" Alex asked.

Sangster said, "Well, for one thing it's the name of a New Wave band."

"What's New Wave?"

Armstrong pursed her lips, a kind of choked smile.

Sangster continued, "But it means the Voice, the Super Voice, I guess."

"Do you have any data on a vampire called the Voice?" Alex asked hopefully.

"We're looking," Armstrong said.

Carreras cleared his throat. "It is time we consider the wisdom of returning Van Helsing to the school. For his own safety."

All were silent.

"Whoa, whoa," said Alex. "And then what? What does that mean? Without a school to go to, I got no reason to be here."

He realized he was bringing to the surface a matter that had not really been discussed. Alex was being trained and allowed to work for the Polidorium because they believed he had something to offer. But would he be working with the Polidorium if he was no longer attending school nearby? Did they value him enough—and that was the way he was thinking of it, as though he were a really great car—to find some excuse to keep him around if he wasn't in school here? The answer had to be absolutely not. No organization was going to just take in a fourteen-year-old. If the school was gone, or he was gone from the school, he was as good as gone to the Polidorium.

"You're not my parents," Alex said when he finally decided on his line of reasoning. "I'll decide if I'm at that school."

Sangster clawed at his own forehead. "If the Scholomance is serious, serious enough to try to get rid of Alex, then he's important to our mission."

Armstrong turned to Carreras. "As much as I hate to say it, I agree. Look, they're already gonna try to kill him every chance they get, so that's nothing new."

"Yeah," said Alex brightly. "That's nothing new."

Armstrong seemed to think of a new angle. "Could this be about Montrose?"

"What's Montrose?" Alex asked.

"That would be the man behind Chatterbox," Sangster said. "And I have no idea if it's related or not."

Carreras nodded and finally said, "We need to find out what this Voice is up to. Alex stays with the school—wherever the school is."

Alex opened his hands, *Whaa?* "I just said it's my decision. . . ."

"Very good, sir," Sangster said.

The supplies Sangster and Alex had to get were actually bigger than the van: a trailer full to the brim of cots and bedding, which they loaded from the dock of a store warehouse in Secheron with the help of various workmen brought in at Otranto's behest.

When they left the warehouse, Alex saw that they were headed out of town. "This isn't the way back to Village Hall," he observed as Sangster drove.

"We're not going back to Village Hall," said the instructor.

"Where are we going?"

"Someplace safe."

Twenty minutes later the van fell in line behind the caravan of buses pulling down a long, manicured drive that Alex recognized. He read the stone sign as they passed it on the driveway.

"LaLaúrie School for Girls," he said thoughtfully. "Of course."

"Our sister school. It's temporary," Sangster said, "just long enough to see what kind of damage the fire caused and get us back open. But this was the only place available."

Sangster drove around the buses and parked in the circular drive at the front of the mansionlike building. Alex blinked in wonder at a strange vision. A line of ten or so old-fashioned oil lanterns threaded out the entrance, held aloft by women and girls in uniform coming down the wide front steps. The light from the lamps danced across the courtyard and his heart leapt at the warmth of the gesture.

As Alex got out of the van, he paused.

Standing on the steps before him, holding up a lantern like a beacon at sea, was Minhi Krishnaswami.

"Welcome," she said.

Chapter 4

Javi and the other RAs were drafted into the service of handing out bedrolls and pillows, and the boys all fell into line. Alex, Sid, and Paul took the bedding that was offered and walked, dazed and exhausted, following like ants into the gymnasium of LaLaurie.

They trudged in silence up into the building. Alex had thought previously that LaLaurie was like "Glenarvon with more flowers," and now, as his shoes echoed on the tile floor and he and Paul caught sight of one or two girls looking past doors that led up into stairwells and private rooms, LaLaurie reminded him of "Glenarvon except not on fire."

"We are in foreign territory now, mate," said Paul.

"Did you get to talk to Minhi?" Alex asked.

"Just for a moment," Paul responded. "She had to get the hot chocolate." Minhi had led the first group inside while Alex and his friends got into line.

Minhi was their friend already. She had come into their lives like one of the manga characters she loved, bending back Bill Merrill's ear to stop a fight that Alex actually would have won anyway. She had defused a violent situation and introduced herself as "Minnie-with-an-h," and they had instantly liked her. Besides all that, she had loaned Sid a stack of books. And then she and Paul had been kidnapped by vampires. The time in captivity had brought her close to Paul, and over the past month the gang—Paul, Sid, Minhi, and Alex, the four who shared the truth—had gathered together whenever they could find an excuse to meet up in town.

The three boys reached the entrance to the gymnasium and Paul let out a slow whistle. "Behold," he said, "the Kingdom of Cots."

The gymnasium had become a kind of hostel, with cots stretching in long rows. Some boys were already asleep, while others were gathering in groups around the cots. Alex saw sooty faces looking back at him all along the way. He was momentarily plagued by guilt at not seeing the loathed Merrill brothers. They were a couple of jerks, but no one deserved what Steven had gotten, and Alex especially didn't like being the reason for it. "It looks like *Gone with the Wind* in here," Alex said, thinking of the makeshift hospitals that had been set up during the American Civil War. He had seen that movie with his mother, who had a weakness for old movies, and he had been struck by the images of public halls being converted this way, with cots and sheets and, in that case and thankfully not this one, doctors with hacksaws.

"Guys!" Minhi beckoned them from a table along the wall, where she was briefly visible through a clustered crowd of boys. Alex saw the steam rising off the Styrofoam cups they held, and he realized she was giving away hot chocolate.

He, Paul, and Sid picked up their step. When they got there, Minhi poured cups and handed one immediately to each of them.

"Thank you," Sid said.

"Absolutely," Minhi said. She reached out and hugged Paul, pecking him on the cheek.

Alex took the kiss Minhi gave Paul in stride. No big deal. Precisely why he wasn't bothered by it. Not at all.

A girl next to Minhi cleared her throat, and Alex turned to the sound of papers rustling. The girl stood up from her place behind the table and said, "Please take one."

"What's all this?" Alex asked as he took the paper. The girl looked up with a tired but patient look. She wore a green, shimmery scarf, tied in a jaunty fashion around her neck. Her hair was brown and chin length, stiff and well arranged.

"This is everything you're going to need to know for the next few days at least," she said with an accent that reminded Alex of a Pedro Almodovar movie, husky and full of strange, slushy s's and y's that sounded like j's: *Thish izh everything jor going to need*. As she spoke, the scarf danced briefly. She swept her arm toward the Kingdom of Cots. "This is where you'll sleep. There's a map on the sheet, and hours when you'll have access to the showers in the back of the gym. We didn't have much time but there are some . . . rules and instructions on what to do about classes." She smiled very slightly, more with her eyes than her mouth.

Sid was looking at the paper. "Yeah, how are we gonna do classes? And where are the instructors sleeping? And—"

"Ah—right now the paper is all we have. If the answer's not there it's because no one's told us yet." Alex noticed that she sounded both compassionate and weary, as though she'd already said this too many times.

"Vienna, these are my friends," Minhi interjected. "This is Alex Van Helsing, Sid Chamberlain, and this is Paul Messina."

"Oh, *this* is Paul," Vienna said, and she flicked her eyes up and down. "*Eso es.*"

"Vienna?" Alex asked.

"This is Vienna Cazorla," said Minhi. "She's my roommate."

"Cazorla," Vienna corrected, hitting the middle *z* with a *th* sound, *Cathorla*. She smiled briefly again, an entrancing and instantly vanishing phenomenon.

Alex tried to think of something good and came up with, "Cazorla, that's Spanish, right?"

She nodded. The eyes again. Wow.

"But yet your first name is Vienna, that's . . . unusual, isn't it?"

"It is a strange world." Vienna shrugged. Then she remembered her list and looked down, checking off the three boys' names. She flipped through it for a moment and glanced up, gazing past them. "Is there no one else?"

"We're the last," Alex said. He started to say something profoundly stupid like *we always save the best for last* and by the grace of God he somehow did not.

"What about . . ." Vienna bit her lip, searching her list.

For a moment Minhi and Vienna turned to each other, and Vienna looked back. "Do you know Steven Merrill?"

Alex felt the blood drain from his face. A jumble of responses flooded into his mind, and he stammered, "You . . . you're looking for Steven?" *The silent terror of Glenarvon? The one who got bitten by a vicious Glimmerhook?*

"I don't see either of them," Vienna said to Minhi. By which she meant the Merrills.

Paul was looking at Minhi, with a sort of *Wha—?* look.

"They haven't come in," said Minhi. "Vienna and Steven are . . ."

"Old friends," Vienna said. "From primary school."

"Oh," Alex said, trying to take in the strange revelation that the Merrills could have friends. He had thought their amusements ran more to the torturing puppies variety. But the arm-swinging joie de vivre had gone out of Vienna.

"Steven's been injured," Alex said finally. "His brother is with him at the hospital."

Vienna's eyes grew wide and she brought her hand to her lips. She flipped the sheets, clearing her throat again. "I'll make a note of it." Abruptly she smiled awkwardly at Minhi and scurried away, disappearing out of the gymnasium entirely.

Paul watched her go. He said to Minhi, "A friend of *yours* is a friend of *theirs*?"

"Do you really want to get into this now?" Minhi asked.

CHAPTER 5

In the Kingdom of Cots the refugees slept fitfully, Alex and Sid and Paul next to one another. Sheets were strung from metal pipes that had been rolled in, making the place look even more like a wartime hospital than it had before.

There were countless basic necessities that everyone was slow to realize he was missing—Alex, for instance, needed contact solution because he'd been wearing his contacts for two days. They were the extended-wear kind; he could keep them in for two weeks if need be, but ever since he'd gotten them he'd been in the habit of taking them out every night, anyway. It went with preparing for bed as surely as did brushing his teeth and changing into pajamas; on went the glasses.

Alex was pretty sure his glasses had melted clean away in the fire. He would need to go into town and get a new prescription and some new glasses, any glasses. Just for some normalcy.

Breakfast in the morning was brought into the Kingdom of Cots on long tables, and Headmaster Otranto addressed them as they filed like zombies through the line for bread and juice.

"This is not a permanent solution," Otranto said.

"Sir, when are we going back to the school?" Javi the RA asked cautiously. Alex leaned against the wall, sipping his orange juice. When indeed.

"Ah, yes," Otranto said. He thrust his hands in his pockets. "It will take some time. There is considerable damage to Aubrey House and the inspectors have only begun to look at it. And unfortunately before we can repair, there are certain requirements that we will have to meet, requirements that we were allowed to ignore as long as no new construction was going on. I'm talking about things you may not keep track of, air conditioning, old insulation in the ceilings. The answer is, months."

Everyone was stunned. Alex looked back at the cots and hanging sheets and the students' looks of horror.

"If we're lucky," Otranto continued. "So. It is time we discuss what we are going to do now. This school,

LaLaurie School, was founded in 1834 by the same American and French investors who founded Glenarvon, converting a number of grand houses left in a patron's will. There is one house that has not been used in over seventy-five years. It has rooms enough to house us. Some of you who have been in double rooms will now be in triples—we can't help that." Alex glanced around again and judged that tripling up might not be necessary: There were already fewer students anyway. Some boys had trickled out in the wee hours. Alex had even seen Fred Schunk, another of the RAs, shaking Otranto's hand, a valet in the hall behind him holding what was left of Fred's stuff.

Another boy, a senior Alex had never met, raised a hand. "Sir? What caused the fire?"

Alex stiffened and shot a look at Sangster, who stood calmly nearby.

Otranto scratched the back of his neck. "It's not final, but I can say that this morning the inspectors brought me a burnt-out electrical plug. So at this point it looks like a wiring mishap."

Alex blinked. Sangster nodded an impossibly tiny nod, a micro-expression that said, *We've got this covered.* The Polidorium: good friends to have, and likely terrible enemies.

Otranto continued, "The Board of Regents at

Glenarvon has released sufficient funds for us to prepare the house to live in. This will be done with workers and with the help of the students, and I trust all of you will volunteer to assist in the effort."

Otranto looked around. "Am I correct?"

Paul whispered, "What do you think that place looks like? A bunch of rotten beds, covered in sheets? If there *are* beds."

"Am I correct?" Otranto said again.

Alex loved the thought of the boys of Glenarvon forced to do manual labor. Loved it. He had spent his life choosing things that didn't fit the family name (the public version, not the secret, thought-to-be-fictional one). He abandoned the violin as soon as he could ditch the lessons, hating the gentility of it and the incessant repetition of "The Children's Waltz." He was expected to learn to sail, and did, though he preferred to use his muscles in other ways, entering more and more dangerous pastimes. He was always amazed that "people like us" would spend hours in a gym but couldn't be bothered to lift a couch. So he was eager to see these guys at work.

Alex leaned forward. "Absolutely."

This broke the silence, and many more boys spoke up.

Otranto was satisfied. "That too is not a permanent

solution. Glenarvon will be repaired. Even now we are assessing the damage. Glenarvon will not die on my watch," he said flatly.

"What do we do now?" Paul called. "What about classes?"

"Class assignments are posted on the board," Otranto said, pointing at a bulletin board that someone had installed overnight. Alex saw rows of yellow legal paper there. "What you do now is get back to being students. We are guests of LaLaurie, but we are Glenarvon still."

Sangster cleared his throat. Otranto looked back and said, "Mr. Sangster will now pass on another word."

Sangster came forward and pointed at a number of giant cardboard boxes on the stage. "Those are uniforms." Alex looked and saw the RAs beginning to haul out hundreds of pairs of slacks, shirts, and sport coats and lay them on the edge of the stage. "In a minute we'll start calling names; come forward and pick up your clothes. If your shoes do not fit, trade or hang tight and we'll get more. You will be issued a footlocker—those are over there—and three uniforms each; laundry day is Thursday. At the end of the line after the uniforms are supplies: towels, T-shirts, underwear. By ten o'clock this morning, I want you all looking like soldiers. Here's why," he said, and stopped, thrusting his hands into his pockets. "We are guests." He repeated the word emphatically. "*Guests.* I don't have time to tell you guys what I mean by that because there are a million things that'll flow through your heads over the next few days, some good, some pretty damn stupid. So remember it: *guests.* We are overwhelming the space, the materials, and likely soon the patience of the ladies of LaLaurie. This means that I am demanding of you that you think at every moment, *Is this what a guest would do?* And if so, *do it*. And if not, I beg of you, *don't.*" He smiled. That gave everyone enough of a release of tension to laugh.

"Yeah, I know. It's an adventure. Keep your cots squared away, do whatever our hosts ask. Be polite, be cool, make friends. I know it doesn't seem like it, but it's all gonna be fine."

Alex got three uniforms that appeared to fit, and a pair of shoes that didn't, so they clopped when he wore them. He wandered around until he found someone whose shoes were too tight, and that was that.

He realized that his possessions now consisted of a towel, pajamas, underwear, and three identical sets of a T-shirt, button-down, pants, and one jacket.

On Monday, with everyone still fumbling around in complete confusion, they were forced to go back to class.

It was a mercifully short half-day schedule, compressed to allow for familiarizing and starting late, with classes coming in half-hour sessions.

At ten o'clock, Paul, Sid, and Alex wandered until they found the right class. The room was crammed full with desks, and they saw Minhi in a row at the back. As they took their seats, Alex understood. Every last class had been shuffled and merged.

Literature was taught together by Sangster and Ms. Daughtry, LaLaurie's assistant headmistress and a lit expert to match Sangster. They didn't alternate sentences or anything; rather Sangster was to lecture on one topic and Daughtry on the other.

"Did you know we'd be in class together?" asked Minhi. Next to her was Vienna, who Alex recognized as much by her faraway look as by the scarf she still wore.

Paul shook his head. "We don't know a bloody thing."

"That is totally true," whispered Alex. "It's insane. We got a speech yesterday telling us not to, I don't know, run around naked or something."

"I would recommend against it." Minhi nodded solemnly.

"I'm thinking it's not something guests would do," said Alex. "But there actually wasn't a list."

Vienna looked up and leaned over. "I will bet you by

the time the week is out? You will have a list."

She speaks, thought Alex, and he thought instantly of Steven Merrill, who was also always silent, and now was—jeez—still in the hospital, he could only assume. He looked around and did not see Bill. For a moment it all came flooding back. And then Ms. Daughtry began to teach.

This wasn't a perfect setup; in lit, Sangster had been teaching *Idylls of the King* and Daughtry had been teaching William Blake's *Songs of Innocence and of Experience.* The guests toed the line: Blake it was. Alex marveled at the idea that while he had been settling into the Kingdom of Cots and Otranto had been calling the ends of the earth to summon hundreds of uniforms, the instructors had been laboring into the night merging their syllabi.

"Those of you from the Glenarvon contingent," said Ms. Daughtry, "may not be familiar with Blake, and I'll spare you the week we just spent on his biography. But the *Songs* has a lot to say about us, as human beings, as thinkers, as students together. Mister Sangster!"

Sangster was seated behind her to the left, thumbing through the book, and looked up as if startled. She didn't look back at him, but continued, "Would you care to share with the class something appropriate from Blake?"

Sangster nodded and rose, thumbing through a copy of the book. "I would choose . . . I would choose . . ."

"You do know the book?" she asked, smiling.

"It's funny," Sangster replied. "I think the message of this morning is 'The Divine Image.'"

Someone cleared his throat. All eyes turned to see Bill Merrill standing in the doorway.

Bill looked haggard—he was still muscular from countless hours at soccer practice and beating smaller students senseless, but his cheeks were hollow and his eyes were lined with mottled blue. Bill handed Sangster an official-looking note, probably from the office, and Sangster nodded. Alex made out, *Like to take a seat?* and Bill slowly made his way to an empty desk.

Vienna sat up with interest and waved at Bill as he sat. She leaned over, whispering about Steven. Bill gestured back with open hands, *I'll tell you later.*

Sangster said, "For those of you who want to send a card to Steven, I think you can give them to Bill. I understand some of the students are organizing a visit if any of you want to go."

Several people patted Bill on the shoulder. Alex was thinking about Steven once coldcocking Paul on the side of the head to distract Alex so Bill could punch him in the nose, and of the Glimmerhook landing on Steven's back.

Ms. Daughtry spoke, bringing the class back to form. They went over Blake, but Alex felt befuddled by the obscene and forced normality of trying to have a class when students were homeless and Steven was in the hospital. He kept dropping into the lecture and then zoning out until finally she said, "Before we wrap I need to catch you all up on the Pumpkin Show."

The what? The boys in class were obviously lost as to the meaning of this, but the girls chattered sotto voce to one another. Ms. Daughtry continued, "This is a LaLaurie tradition, so those of you who are new get a chance to join us at our best—well, our best next to Christmas."

Minhi whispered to Sid, "You're going to love this."

"Starting this week, with available slots after school, students will be presenting original works—generally written, but if you choose you can sign up to sing, dance, display a collage; it doesn't matter. The theme is the autumn season."

"You mean like Halloween?" Sid asked, a little too excitedly. "Like, vampires and ghosts?"

Daughtry opened her hands. "Whatever suits. Vampires, ghosts, meandering stories about the decay of the fall; we get a fair amount of those. The theme is the season; the prize is the Plaque," she said almost wistfully. "Next to the library you'll find a case displaying the names of our winners going back to 1945. It's like a harbinger of success; every single winner has gone on to great things. Not that there's any pressure." Ms. Daughtry smiled. "Performances will be voted on by the attendees."

"Performances," Sid muttered, slumping a little. He clearly liked the idea of writing, but reading aloud sounded a bridge too far.

"Come on," said Alex. "You could do that." At least, Alex thought so. Sid seemed to spend every moment writing something or other, most of it descriptions of characters from his vampire games. Alex had never met anyone who carried around so much information on one subject—if it might be called a subject—in his head.

"We start reading on Tuesday, so get those stories written and those monologues practiced and get your names on the sign-up sheets," Daughtry concluded. And with that, class was over.

As the class filed out, Alex turned to Sid excitedly. "This is a *great* idea, man."

"I've never read a story aloud before," Sid said. "I've never even written that kind of story."

"You've written whole books on that vampire game," Paul said.

"Those are more like articles," Sid protested. "They're in a folder where you already know the game. This is . . . harder."

Alex watched Vienna go talk to Bill, who glared at Alex hatefully but then softened when he talked to her.

"Well, *I* do this every year," Minhi said. "I mean, I don't get anywhere, but you'll love it. Everyone reads from a big chair in the library, surrounded by candles. They move the chair for the singers and actors to perform."

"Oh my God, I don't have any of my articles and books," said Sid, thinking of the items Paul had mentioned. "All that stuff is gone." He looked ill suddenly, as though he'd forgotten.

"We'll go into town," Minhi said. "It'll be fun. We'll get some new stuff, maybe some books on how to write a story. Hey, I could use some actual instructions." She smiled encouragingly. "Huh?"

Sid nodded and Paul folded his arms. "That sounds perfect."

Minhi turned to Vienna, who was approaching as she moved away from Bill. "Vienna, you up for a trip to Secheron?"

"Anything to get out of here," she said.

They got up and neared the front of the class, where

Ms. Daughtry was erasing things on the chalkboard. A cloud of chalk dust rose and scattered, and Alex coughed. He felt a speck or two get into his eye. He squinted and rubbed at his eyelid.

"What is it?" Minhi asked.

"*Ow*—I got—" Alex doubled over, leaning on the desk. He could feel the specks swimming over his eyeball. His eye sang out with pain and he felt the plastic lens begin to wrinkle. "I got chalk in my contact."

"Does it hurt?" Paul asked. Alex held up a hand, both in agony and almost wanting to laugh.

"Jeez—" He reached his fingers toward his eye. He needed the contact out right away.

"Do you have any solution?" Vienna asked, already rooting through her bag.

"Do you?" Minhi asked her.

"Not here."

"I don't have any," Alex said. "I need to get some. Don't worry, gimme a second, I can use spit."

"Ew," Minhi said.

Alex winced as he started to pry open his eye, and then felt it shut in defiance. "Please, don't make me laugh."

"Good Lord," Vienna said, "come with me."

Still slightly hunched, Alex felt her take his sleeve and

guide him out of the room. They walked down the hall and he heard the footsteps of the others behind him. It never ceased to amaze him how delicate the eye was, and how easily he could be rendered nearly powerless with a few specks of dust. It was the equivalent of bending someone's pinkie back—just a little bit of pressure and the subject is subdued. "Hang on, I can just take it out and hold it in my mouth."

"Don't be ridiculous," she said. "I have solution in my room."

They reached a doorway on the floor level and Vienna stopped for a second, seeming to stare at the door as though she needed a key.

"He can't go up there," Minhi said behind them.

"Eh." Vienna scoffed. "You three wait here."

Up a short flight of stairs onto a second level, and suddenly Alex was in a different world, a hallway of wooden floors and throw rugs and warmly painted walls.

A girl in a robe was coming out of a bathroom and whispered, "Are you insane?" to Vienna, who rushed him to a door halfway down the hall.

Still blinking, Alex was barely able to take in the room. He made out two beds opposite each other. The two halves of the room were very different—one was done up in bright colors, and Alex made out blurred stacks of manga next to the bed. That must be Minhi's.

Vienna's half of the room reminded him in a blink of a madhouse for some reason, but he only had a moment to look before she led him to a vanity mirror and sink.

He washed his hands and pried his right eye open, pinching his thumb and forefinger against his eyeball. "Okay," he said. Next to him, Vienna was rooting through various bottles around the sink. "Argh!" Alex hissed as the contact swam away from his fingers and slipped clean under his eyelid.

He tried to pry his eye open once more. Through the pain he became aware that she was clearing her throat, leaning patiently against the sink. He pressed his face very close to the mirror, trying to see the thin edge of the contact against the red eyeball. "Here," Vienna said. She took him by the shoulders and turned him toward her. "Open your eye. Hold it open." He relented and did what she said.

"Turn your eye around," she said, and he was struck again by the cadence and throaty quality of her accent, *Torn jor aiyy arond.* "You know, all around. Now look down."

Her delicate thumb and forefinger, their colored nails somehow avoiding the tender flesh of his eyeball, came close and in one swift movement plucked the contact from his eye.

She smiled, holding out the contact, and placed it in the palm of his hand. Then she handed him the lens solution.

"Thank you," he said, holding the contact. His eye was red and he brought the contact up, his face very close to the mirror. He couldn't bear to put it back in. Not right away, anyway. "Gimme a second."

Vienna clicked her tongue. "How long have you been wearing contacts?"

"A couple of months," he said. "You?"

"About the same, but you seem to have a more complicated relationship with them."

Alex had to laugh, careful not to drop the contact, which was swimming in a small puddle of solution in the palm of his hand.

"They may not be correctly fitted," said Vienna.

"That or I'm just pathetic," he said ruefully. He looked at her, drawn once more to the scarf around her neck. The décor that had said "madhouse" to him caught his good eye in the mirror and he turned around, looking at the walls on her side.

What had looked at first like a padded wall was in fact a wall of white sheets of paper with pencil sketches on them. He couldn't make them out very well from across the room. "What is all that?"

"Those?" Vienna said, the way someone might say, *this old thing?* "Oh, they change out all the time. It's whatever I'm working on."

"For class?" Alex asked. Now he took the contact in his fingers and leaned in close to the mirror. He placed the contact back in his eye. He braced for a little bit of pain, since the eye was still sore, but swirled his eye around and the contact stuck.

"Not all of them," she was saying.

After a moment Alex turned back and stepped closer to the wall over her bed. Indeed, they were pencil sketches, some of them clearly figure drawings for some art class or another, a few still lifes. But an entire two columns of sheets were broken up into squares, panels, and he caught images of characters with big eyes and spiky hair. "This is manga," he said.

"They're Minhi's," Vienna said when he looked at her.

"She drew these?"

"No, she does the stories, the plots. I'm working on the art."

"You're doing a manga together?" He smiled, studying the characters. Now he could see the similarity—the pencil strokes in the subway stations and form of the hands of the characters did indeed look to be from the same creator as the more classical images. "That's really seriously cool."

He blinked again and she came close, peering at his eye. "It's very red. Do you need to just take it out for the day?"

"I lost my glasses," Alex said. "And I really like to see." She was very close.

Someone cleared her throat and Alex looked at Minhi, who had come into the room. Minhi waved. "Get it all worked out?"

Alex nodded vigorously. "Oh, yeah, I'll live."

"Then you need to get out of here before we all get kicked out," Minhi said. "Come on, the coast is clear."

As they headed down the hall, Minhi and Vienna whispered inaudibly behind him. Alex couldn't make out any of it. As they emerged into the main hall, Paul accosted him.

"How was the forbidden zone?" Paul asked.

"Surprisingly manga-esque," Alex answered.

As Alex walked ahead he heard Paul say to Sid, "See, mate? I told you he wears them for the girls."

Chapter 6

La Librairie Fahey lay on a side street of the village square in Secheron, and though it was not vast like the book superstores Alex knew in the States, it seemed bigger on the inside than from the outside. Alex and Sid meandered through its three narrow stories looking for reference material, up and down wooden stairs that were themselves lined with shelves. On the second floor the staircase opened out into a small café, where a number of visitors sipped espresso and pored over their books. As they moved up to the third floor, Alex paused, tilting a head for Sid's benefit. "*Birks*," he whispered.

"What?"

"Birks. It's what my sisters and I call all the random

guys in Birkenstock sandals."

Sid looked, and Alex silently indicated a blond guy with dreadlocks and the eponymous sandals. "You don't like Birkenstocks? They're, like, totally comfortable."

Alex nodded as they climbed. "They are that. What's the blond guy reading?"

Sid peered down.

"It's, uh—"

"Don't tell me. *L'Étranger.*"

"No . . ."

"*À la Recherche du Temps Perdu.*"

"Wow!" Sid marveled. "How do you do that?"

"Birkwatching, man," Alex said, shaking his head. "Travel around enough, you gotta do something with your time." He saw a paper sign tacked near the staircase that said, LIVRES EN ANGLAIS / ENGLISH BOOKS, and tapped it.

The third floor was better lit than the second, with some love seats and wooden chairs and a cushioned bay window that looked out on the street below. Past the bestsellers and necessary English translations of Camus and Proust they found collections of short stories.

"What are we looking for, exactly?" Sid asked.

"I have no idea. I probably would have done better with *your* library," Alex said.

"My library is gone with the wind." Sid shook his head in sadness.

"Oh God, I'm sorry," said Alex. "I can't believe I keep forgetting that." Sid had had two shelves of books, many of them nonfiction, but he had reams of vampire novels and stories. He was a connoisseur of all things vampire and was in the process of creating stacks of character sheets for a game that as far as Alex knew no one else at Glenarvon played—Scarlet World, a role-playing game about vampires. Sid liked to dig deep into primary texts, old stories. "I never rip off a movie unless I can find a book to back it up," he had explained, and Alex wasn't sure what that meant but it seemed to mean something to Sid. Everyone had a hobby.

Sid scanned the floor-to-ceiling shelf in front of him. "These are stories, but—if we have to write something, I mean—we need something about, you know, *how* to write, don't we?"

They began to move around the shelf when they heard someone say, "That's *brilliant*," in a pronounced British accent. As Alex and Sid stepped into the Language Arts section, they saw Paul, who was rummaging through books with Minhi and joshingly fighting over one.

"I spotted this!" Minhi said.

"But it's called *Master Plots*," said Paul. "As in, all the plots. In one book."

"What did you find?" Alex asked. Behind Minhi, he saw Vienna, wearing her jaunty green scarf.

Minhi turned around, letting Paul have the book with a shake of her head. "Hey, guys!"

"We're looking for something to help us write a story," said Paul. "And we just found one called *Master Plots*."

"Can I see that?" Sid asked, taking it. He thumbed through, showing it to Alex. Inside were countless outlines: "The Romance," "The Action Story," "The Mystery." Sid shrugged indecisively.

"There's another one here," said Vienna, taking another copy off the shelf.

"I don't know," said Sid.

"What is it you were hoping to find?" Vienna asked him. Her eyes ran past Alex, and Alex felt himself trying to make eye contact, feeling mildly crushed that she failed to connect.

"Sid's something of a purist," said Alex. "He reads old books, old stories. Am I right?" He looked at his Canadian friend.

"Something like that. I guess I'm looking for something less—mercenary." Sid shrugged again.

Vienna scanned the books. Her scarf danced a little

as she eyed something on the top shelf. She reached up to take the book, bouncing slightly on the balls of her feet. She pulled down a tattered, leather-bound book, inspecting it for a moment, and then turned around. "What do you think of this?"

Sid took it, reading the cover. "Do you know this book?"

"I just thought it looked old," she said, smiling.

Sid read the title aloud. "*The Skein: A Study of Narrative Form*, by David Cracknell." The book seemed to wheeze and crack as he opened it and he began gingerly flipping pages.

> *The short story, unlike the novel, allows no freedom to lose the rhythm that is key to every moment. Rhythm finds its way into the reader's mind, and the author fails if he does not maintain it.*

Sid looked up. "It's a theory book."

"*Está bien*," said Vienna. "We tried."

"No, no," Sid said, smiling. He seemed relieved. "No, this is the one for me."

"Way to go," said Alex to Vienna, and she curtsied slightly, jokingly. Paul and Minhi were reading through their own *Master Plots* books, and Alex began to search the shelves, looking for something that might call to him the same way. But his heart wasn't in it. In truth he had no intention of giving the story competition more than a cursory effort. There was too much going on in the off-hours. There was Ultravox, after all.

He turned, opening his mouth to ask Vienna if she would be entering the contest, and discovered she was no longer standing there.

Alex looked across the room and saw Vienna in front of the bay window, looking out into the street. Alex grabbed another copy of *Master Plots* off the shelf and walked over.

"So what about you?" he asked.

She didn't respond, and Alex followed her eyes through the window, moving closer to look down to the cobblestone streets below.

Someone was standing across the street, stock-still and staring up at the window.

Her again. Elle wore black pants and boots and a pair of dark glasses, and had a white leather coat pulled close and tied with a belt.

Alex darted his eyes to Vienna, who had not diverted her gaze. "Do you know that girl?" he said softly.

Vienna spoke low after a second and he saw her scarf dance. "No."

Elle pursed her lips in a smile. She had spotted him.

"Tell the others I had to run," Alex said. He launched himself down the stairs, past the café, and onto the first floor. He slammed past shoppers in line at the checkout counter and hurtled outside, aware of the sound of the bells jingling on the door.

All up and down the street, people moved slowly, hands thrust in their pockets against the October chill. Elle was no longer there.

Alex looked down the block and saw the white coat disappearing around a corner. He ran for it.

Elle could be insanely fast. If Alex had seen her disappearing around a corner, there was a good chance it was because she was toying with him. So be it.

Alex turned onto an avenue called Matthias, which was lined with dark wood, bars, and restaurants. People were gathering, meeting one another for early dinner. As the street sloped down he saw it terminate at the docks of the marina, the gray water of the lake yawning in the distance.

There she was, running faster now, headed for the docks.

By the time Alex reached the docks, he had lost her. He nodded at a yacht's captain as he stepped out onto one of the narrow jetties, moving past a myriad of small craft, the sound of wind and the clanking of boats and lines filling the air.

What was she doing here? Alex ran through all that he knew about her from when he had faced her before, in the hidden school called the Scholomance. Was she watching for him? She had been staring at Vienna, though. Or she had been staring up and Vienna had spotted her. *Spotted* was an obvious and inexact word in this case—Elle had been standing out like a sore and bone white thumb; she had wanted to be seen.

Alex stepped along the boards, feeling the chill against his sport coat. He reached the end of the pier and turned left, looking around him, moving along a walk that led to other piers of the marina. A stone picnic table sat up ahead, a long, thick umbrella still piercing down through the center of it. The blue cloth of the umbrella fluttered, and he reached out to move it aside.

As he touched the umbrella, a white hand reached around and grabbed his wrist.

Alex saw his own reflection in Elle's Italian sunglasses as she dragged him off his feet, swinging him off the pier for a moment and around. She let go and he hit the boards, rolling and sliding, catching the brunt with his shoulders.

He got to his feet and into the warrior stance Sangster

had taught him, half turned, weight evenly distributed, toes curled to provide extra balance, one foot forward.

"Why are you following me?" he demanded.

She stopped, putting her hands in her coat pockets, spiky blond hair lifting in the wind. As she smiled, her fangs showed. Elle's teenage look notwithstanding, there was no telling her age. She was out in the late daylight, so she could handle some sun. That meant she could be hundreds of years old, he had learned. The Polidorium hadn't told him that—Sid had, because when it came to knowing about vampires, the redheaded Canadian had some game.

"At this point it looks like you're following me," Elle said, shrugging.

Alex looked around. He wasn't carrying any weapons. That didn't necessarily mean he couldn't handle her—without weapons he had defeated vampires before—but the odds were against him. And he had too many questions. If she wanted to talk, he was more than interested. He relaxed his stance a little, holding up his hands. "Why did you try to poison me?"

"Poison? Are you talking about the worms?" she responded. "Well, naturally because the Scholomance wants you *dead*."

"You say it like you're not a part of them."

She seemed to blur for a second and suddenly she was behind him, her arm wrapped around him, her dead hand up under his chin. Not squeezing. Just making a point. "Oh, I'm a part of them, boy. But let me tell you how this goes. They want you dead because they consider you a *threat* the way *nits* turn into *lice*. They don't want you to suffer; they want you out of the way."

Alex grabbed her wrist and twisted, moving away, and she let him. Then she grabbed him by the shoulders and slammed him against a metal pole.

"But that's just being shortsighted, Alex," said Elle. "I actually would *prefer* that you suffer. At least a little."

"Why? Because of my freaking *name*?" Alex brought up his knees and smashed at her leather-bound torso with his shoes, sending her backward. He scuttled in the opposite direction, moving farther away and into a fighter stance again. This was insane. She could rip out his throat any time she wanted, and she wasn't even trying.

He edged back against the umbrella and the table, ready to either fight or turn and head for the mainland.

"You don't know who you're screwing with," she said through bared teeth. "And I'm not letting you destroy what's left of my life. Tell me—what do *you* care about?"

Alex was struck by the strangeness of what she was saying. This sounded personal, and that made no sense at all. "Care is a big word coming from you," Alex said. "You said yourself that you guys don't give a damn about anyone, isn't that right? No empathy, no love?"

There was a rapid plodding of footsteps up the marina, and Alex heard someone calling his name. Alex glanced past the poles to the main pier and saw his friends. Minhi, Paul, Sid, and Vienna were coming down the dock, splitting up. He saw Paul and Minhi go off on one trail, Sid another. Vienna was coming his way. In a moment she would reach the end of the pier and she'd be able to see him.

Vienna reached the end and turned left, and suddenly she was staring at Alex and Elle. She backed up instinctively, stopping at the edge of the water.

"What about this one?" Elle said, looking beyond him with a knowing smirk, her eyes invisible behind the glasses.

Suddenly she lunged, breaking into a jaguarlike run; he actually caught a blur of her nails reaching all the way down to the boards of the dock as she moved, and as she drove past him it felt like he had been sideswiped by a train.

"No!" Alex shouted, turning. Vienna was frozen at the end of the dock. Alex was running after Elle, trying to catch up, but the vampire was too fast.

Vienna hadn't had time to move a step when Elle

sliced by her, a small cloud of material puffing into the air as she ripped half of the girl's sleeve away.

And then with a barely audible splash the vampire in the white leather coat was gone. Alex was running to the edge of the dock. He saw Vienna twisting, about to fall backward, and he caught her.

Holding Vienna by the waist, he looked past her, searching the water.

Elle was nowhere to be seen.

Alex became aware of Vienna suddenly—she was shaking. He moved her a few steps from the edge and held up his hands. "It's okay," he said. He looked back at the water and started searching the surrounding area. He was thinking he might catch her climbing up somewhere else.

This doesn't happen. That was what his father used to say about anything paranormal, any movie about monsters or vampires or zombies. *Doesn't happen.* For a moment, Alex wished he could go back to the days when he clung to that mantra.

Paul, Sid, and Minhi came running up. "Bloody hell!" Paul shouted. "That was that—that—"

Alex turned to Sid. "Did you see?"

"Absolutely I saw," Sid said, eyes wide. "She jumped in the water."

Vienna was still shaking, staring at her sleeve. "What—"

"I didn't know they could do that," Alex said, frowning. According to lore, and according to Sid, vampires could be killed by holy water but were allergic to any running water, and would seek to avoid crossing it. They certainly wouldn't jump into it.

Sid looked troubled to be caught off guard. "Well, you know, I guess the deal is this is a lake, so it's standing water. As opposed to running."

Minhi touched Vienna on the shoulder. Vienna screamed.

"Hey," Alex said, snapping his attention back to her. "Did she get—are you hurt?" He looked from her sleeve to her face, the giant brown eyes staring at him. She was holding her arm close to her body. "I'm gonna touch your arm, okay?" She nodded.

Alex gingerly took her forearm and brought it forward, glancing over it. Her olive skin was slightly pale and blotchy from cold and fear. "Okay. It's—she didn't leave a scratch," he said. He looked at the others and back at Vienna. "It's okay; I do this all the time."

Minhi rolled her eyes. "Let's go," she said, and hugged Vienna.

Paul and Sid turned their attention back to the water.

"You think there's one o' those entrances right here?"

"Not on the surface," Sid said. "I think she swam to it."

Alex looked back toward the village. "We should go."

Alex took off his sport coat and handed it to Vienna. She stared at the coat for a second, then slipped her own off and put his on, silently.

Now Alex felt cold, but valiantly so.

As they walked up the pier, Minhi was talking to Vienna. "We'll tell you all about it," she said. "As soon as we get you warm."

Paul looked out at the water. "They must waterproof the bloody heck out of those leather jackets."

Chapter 7

Alex took a deep breath. "Vampires are all around the lake," he said.

They'd gathered in an old study in what was now-nicknamed New Aubrey House. The sound of thumping and hammering echoed through the building. They had passed countless students on the way in, and Alex had been happy to see them carrying chairs and bedding from the trucks that were parked all over the lawn. Otranto had set up a small office, a central nervous system for the house, and was running everything from there.

A sign-up sheet near Otranto's office door, posted next to a desk already inhabited by his assistant, Mrs.

Hostache, informed Alex and his roommates that they would be on duty painting and sweeping the next day.

"The sign-up sheet seems to have a mind of its own," Paul observed.

So this was the new reality. Alex had only the faintest inkling of what an undertaking it must be, what kind of money had to change hands and what armies of lawyers had to be called in for two schools to merge so quickly. He had the impression, amid the crates and trucks, of Headmaster Otranto stretching to hold a school together with his bare hands. Alex wasn't sure even Otranto was up to the task. Out of two hundred students they had shed at least twenty-five already.

There was a love seat in the library where Vienna sat shivering, even though Minhi had found a blanket for her. Sid brought in a tray of cups and hot chocolate.

"All of you knew about them?" Vienna asked. She took the chocolate in both hands, absorbing its warmth as she held it under her chin.

Alex indicated Minhi, Paul, and Sid, and said, "All of *us*? Yes," he said. "But I'm not sure if anyone else does, among the students." He looked at the others for help. He wasn't sure how much to reveal. How far to go—*yes, there are vampires, one of those things my father always said didn't exist, and by the way, they have a giant school under the lake, and while we're at it, I've more or less weaseled my way into an international G.I. Joe organization. . . .*

Vienna gestured with her head toward the door, toward the grounds. "Last month, during the kidnapping—I'm sorry to bring it up—"

"No, it's okay," said Minhi. That would be Minhi and Paul's kidnapping by what everyone in the school understood to be terrorists.

"Some of the girls said the terrorists moved fast, very fast." Vienna's eyes were searching. "I didn't see any of it. Were they—were they these things, these vampires?"

"Yes." Minhi nodded.

"Does the school know?"

Alex shrugged. "I don't think the *school* knows," he said. "Glenarvon, I mean. But we do have a friend in the school."

"What about LaLaurie?" Minhi asked. "Does your friend have 'friends' in *our* school?"

Our school. That was the other thing people were trying not to talk about. LaLaurie was traditionally a girls' school. It had its own concerned parents, parents of students whose school *hadn't* been nearly burned down, and they needed soothing, too. They were bending over backward to help Glenarvon, and that meant everything about LaLaurie was having to change. There were boys in the cafeteria and boys in the locker rooms and boy clothes and boy aggression. Boy angst, because their school had been almost destroyed.

Alex shook his head. "I've never asked." It hadn't occurred to him whether there were other Sangsters. Could there be more like him, teachers moonlighting as agents against darkness? That didn't seem likely. Otranto was "connected," but he didn't seem connected to the Polidorium. Ms. Daughtry was kind, and he had a suspicion that Sangster and she might have something going on, but he didn't take her for a spy. But that was how it worked, right? His head began to spin with paranoia.

Vienna turned to Alex, shrugging out of his jacket and handing it back to him. "The girl *knew* you. She was looking for *you*."

Paul chuckled. "That maniac knows all of us. She was our guard when we were taken."

Vienna continued, "But she really knew Alex. What did she want with you?"

"Her name is Elle," Alex said. "And, honestly, I'd tell you if I knew, but I have no idea what she wanted."

Paul asked, "What did she say?"

"She said the Scholomance wants me dead," Alex confessed. He decided to gloss over the punishment part.

At the dock he had been terrified that Elle was going to tear Vienna's throat out, scarf and all. He couldn't handle that; it would have been as if he had lured her down to the dock only to be killed. She would have died because these things seemed to follow him. Already he sensed he was bringing danger to his friends—after all, the school had burned because the Scholomance was *out to get Alex*. But Elle had shot right past Vienna. She had wanted to impart a message. Whatever the Scholomance had planned, they weren't about to trip it up by killing a student in public.

But there was definitely something strange going on that Alex couldn't quite place. Elle had talked as though she were in some kind of disagreement with the Scholomance—whether to kill him or to torture him, apparently. But they had stepped up their attacks on him at the same time that the Scholomance began to prepare for whatever was coming, whatever this Ultravox would bring.

The Scholomance had been around for hundreds—possibly thousands—of years. Dracula himself attended the school, when he first became a vampire, or so said the Polidorium, and so had reported Abraham Van Helsing, Alex's great-great-great- (that was *three* greats) grandfather. Alex had seen the Scholomance personally, as had Paul and Minhi when they had been kidnapped as part of an elaborate vampire plan. The Scholomance had plans within plans within plans.

"Elle wanted me," Alex said. "She didn't want to hurt you, I think, or . . . or she would have." Of course, Elle had actually said she wanted to make Alex suffer, and the truth was, making people suffer often involved hurting others. But he didn't say any of that for now.

Vienna took this in and sipped her chocolate, seeming to relax. "I guess I should say thank you," she said finally.

Alex became aware that someone was yelling down the hall outside the study. Paul went to the door and looked out.

Alex asked, "What is it?"

"It's Bill," Paul said.

Alex stepped past him into the hall, looking down the dim, cobwebby corridor. In the main foyer he saw Bill Merrill, waving a cell phone. "I did try! I did try!"

Otranto said something in a hushed tone, using his hands slowly, palms down, as if to calm the boy. "And we are trying as well."

"I want answers; this is *ridiculous*," Bill said. Abruptly he looked down the hall, catching sight of Alex. He turned instantly and began advancing toward Alex and Paul. "Have you called home?" he shouted at Paul.

Paul seemed confused by the question. "What? Yeah, several times."

"With your cell phone?"

Paul said slowly, "Yeah, you need to borrow it?"

Bill waved his hand. "Agh. England. You! Did you call home?"

"With his phone, but there wasn't a problem," Alex said.

Bill turned back to Otranto, shouting. "You get through. I'm not gonna stand for this."

"What's going on?" Alex asked.

"Stay out of this," Bill said, shooting him a snarling look.

Otranto was leading Bill outside. Alex had a sick, sympathetic feeling in his gut. Bill might be a jerk, but he was just like the rest of them in that he was a student and in theory he had parents somewhere. Every student's parents were putting pressure on their sons, trying to decide whether to stay or to go. But if Alex was understanding Bill correctly, he hadn't been able to contact his parents at all. With Steven in the hospital, that sounded like a nightmare.

Alex and Paul reentered the study as a clock in a high tower over the school began to chime, a quarter to eight. Minhi began to gather up the cups.

Alex asked, "What do you want to do now?"

Minhi shrugged. "Uh . . . well, it's nearly eight. Vienna, are you up for rehearsal?"

"Rehearsal for what?" Alex was puzzled.

Minhi looked at Paul. "You still on?"

"Rehearsal for what?" Alex and Sid said together. Suddenly there was something only half of them were aware of?

Paul looked down, rubbing the back of his neck. "Did I not—it's . . . it's a little stupid."

"It's not stupid." Minhi frowned.

"It's a BALL," Paul said, looking to Alex for sympathy.

"You're going to a ball?" Alex smiled. "Like a . . . pumpkins-and-carriages-and-tuxedos ball?"

Minhi laughed. "A *rehearsal*, Alex, I mean, seriously, do you think there'd be a ball tonight and you'd somehow miss that fact? It's on Friday."

Alex allowed that that had to be true; he could pretty well ignore most of the goings-on at this new, weirdly merged school, but yeah, if there were a big dance tonight there would at least be . . . streamers. Or something.

Vienna brightened. "This Friday there will be a benefit ball for LaLaurie. It includes a debut of the daughters of governmental ministers here for the InfoTreaty."

"InfoTreaty?"

Sid looked up. "Oh, yeah. That's an international

treaty to modernize biographical information and make it easier to share."

Alex said, "How does that translate into a . . . dance?"

Minhi nodded. "There's an international conference on the treaty in Geneva this month, attended by government officials from around the world. The Ball is a black-tie event timed to coincide with that. Of course the talk now is that it'll also be used to raise money for the reconstruction of Glenarvon in addition to the LaLaurie endowment, since the schools were founded by the same board."

Alex was trying to put this together. "A debut of daughters—Minhi, do you have a parent who's like a government minister?"

"Deputy minister," Minhi responded.

"Your dad?"

"My *mom*."

"And my father," Vienna piped up.

"Okay, I get it," Alex said. Really this wasn't so shocking; Glenarvon and LaLaurie were a couple of the most prestigious boarding schools in the world. "So this is a big deal. Is there a ballroom at LaLaurie?"

"We do *have* a ballroom," Vienna said, "so the rehearsals are here. But the actual event . . ."

"It's going to be on a *boat*," Minhi finished excitedly.

"A *boat*?"

"A big one. On the lake." She seemed to bounce.

Alex still didn't get something. "Why do you have to *rehearse*?"

"*Well*," Vienna explained, "you don't just show up and know how to walk down a flight of stairs and dance."

"You don't know how to walk down a flight of stairs?" Alex and Sid folded their arms and looked at their roommate, and Alex said accusingly to him, "How do *you* figure into this?"

"Immunscorrrr," Paul muttered.

"What was that, I couldn't . . ." Alex shook his head, laughing. Minhi raised an eyebrow.

"I'm an escort," Paul said finally. "Every debutante has an escort."

"Technically, junior debutantes," Minhi said. "We don't make a formal debut; we're introduced, but the focus will be on the true debs, the older girls."

True debs. This was a strange new taxonomy. Wow. Minhi and Paul at the ball, that was . . . "Why didn't you mention this?"

Minhi looked sheepish. "Tonight is the first rehearsal. And we didn't . . . there wasn't really an opportunity."

At once flush with the same tinge of jealousy he had felt before, Alex looked at Minhi. He got it. Slightly serious step, sort of romantic, heck, very romantic. He got it. They hadn't mentioned it because they were afraid he'd be jealous. Or, let's face it, because they simply had plans and not everything revolved around Alex Van Helsing.

Alex looked at Vienna. "What about you? Who's your escort, the prince of Spain?"

Vienna glanced down, saddened. "My escort is in the hospital."

Ah. Steven Merrill. Alex thought again of Steven, the one casualty of the fire, and determined that he needed to go see how he was doing. He felt responsible. "I'm sorry." He shook his head honestly. "Jeez, I'm sorry."

"No, it's okay," she said.

"We'll need to find her an escort, Alex," Minhi said meaningfully.

See how this works? She's giving you a shot. Go ahead, make up for putting your foot in your mouth at every opportunity.

Alex's cell phone started buzzing in his pocket. He took it out and read a text that displayed on the screen:

`You're needed. Back gate. 8 P.M.`

Alex blinked at the message and he felt an electric flood pulse through his body. He cleared his throat. "Well, uh, you guys have—I hope it goes great. I have to study, I've completely lost my way in Sangster's class." He looked at Paul and Sid.

Minhi understood, but she looked a little saddened. "Remember you don't have to give *us* that stuff."

"Yeah, okay," Alex said. "It's Sangster."

"All right," Minhi said finally. "We're rehearsing. Sid? You want to come?"

Sid looked as though he'd been jumped. "Me?"

Alex was rising. He had to head back to the Kingdom of Cots and get his go package and his Bluetooth. "I think Vienna needs an escort."

"Excuse me, I do have a say in this," Vienna said, amused. "Sid, would you be my escort for the evening?"

"I have no idea what that—"

"Just come with us and we'll tell you what to do."

Alex smiled, but to do so he had to force the ends of his mouth up. *He* wanted to learn how to walk down a flight of stairs. "Go crazy, Prince." Alex slapped Sid on the back. "I gotta hustle."

Vienna looked at Alex. "Oh, Alex—Ah. My grandmother."

He turned. "Your what?"

"My name *is* unusual. It's Austrian. My grandmother was named Vienna," she said.

Alex felt himself blush despite himself. "Thank you."

Chapter 8

Alex was standing alone at the gate for only about thirty seconds when he heard the sound of a van approaching. In the darkness it was invisible at first, coming around the bend, and then he saw the shape of a black Polidorium van bearing down on him. It pulled between him and the gate—he had to step out of the way to give it a few feet of room, though he suspected the driver had measured his space with expert accuracy—and the van slowed to a stop.

A side door rolled open and Sangster was inside with a headset on, motioning quickly. "Come on, come on."

The slam of a door and they were zipping into the darkness again, no lights, the road illuminated by night vision on the windshield.

"What's all this?" Alex asked.

Armstrong swiveled around in the passenger seat up front and addressed them both. "Alex, we haven't yet had an appropriate time to actually ask you to do something for us, but there's an opportunity coming up that calls for your special—skills."

"I know you're not talking about my awesome karaoke skills," Alex said.

"Ultravox is on a train," Armstrong said. She was surveying a wide printout—a schematic of some kind—and folded it, setting it on her lap. "After days of chatter, Polidorium agents spotted several vampires, security types, the types that guard an important figure, getting off the English Channel ferry and disappearing into a train station in Calais, France. That's where we lost them. But the Scholomance is expecting the crew—they've prepared a meal to greet him; we picked up a call for human gang leaders to turn over members they'd like to get rid of, calls to kidnap, etc. By our estimation Ultravox and his entourage crossed into Switzerland this afternoon, and the Scholomance is expecting them to reach Lake Geneva tonight by train."

Alex felt that adrenaline rush again and instantly scanned the van for materials. He spotted a go package netted to the wall behind Sangster. "Is that where we're headed—we're gonna grab him in Geneva?"

"They never make it to Geneva," Sangster said, and Alex felt the van lurch as it took a hairpin turn. "Every time we have one of these high-level visitors, they jump before they reach Geneva Station."

"Icemaker came in with his own caravan," said Alex, remembering the miles of trucks and other vehicles on the road when the clan lord came to the Scholomance.

"Icemaker was moving a whole army; whereas Ultravox is a high-level operative," Sangster explained, "a sort of master consultant. A string puller. He'll be in the luxury cars. So if we know he'll get off before Geneva—and he will, because they'll leap and head for some magical entrance to the Scholomance—"

"I might have something on that," Alex interrupted, thinking of Elle diving headlong into the water. The water hadn't opened up right there, no magic door—meaning whatever door she headed for was not on the surface.

Sangster leaned forward, and there was an edge of delight in his voice that Alex had never observed before. "Alex, with you—with *you*—we just might be able to catch one of the masters before he jumps."

Alex looked from one agent to the other. So this was the measure of his value to the Polidorium now; he was a vampire detector. *Good enough for me.*

"Where are we going?" Alex asked. Before Sangster could answer he felt himself thrown violently sideways as the van pulled into the driveway of what appeared to be a park or soccer field.

"Let's go," Sangster said. Armstrong slid out of the passenger seat and pulled open the side door. Outside, the air thrummed with the loud, whipping sound of a helicopter dropping onto the field.

"We're going to Zimeysa Station!" Sangster said as they ran. "Keep your head down."

The three of them crossed the forty yards or so to the waiting Black Hawk, which, like the van, bore a Polidorium emblem on its flank. "Why the chopper?" Alex yelled.

"It's forty-five miles west," Sangster shouted back. "We need every second we can get."

Alex had ridden in helicopters before—he and his sister had tagged along numerous times on rescue flights in the mountains of Wyoming—but the Black Hawk was a different affair. The heavy craft rumbled and ripped off the deck and suddenly they were shooting west. Alex was strapped into a seat along the wall.

"Alex! Look alive," Armstrong shouted from where she sat across from him. Behind her in the distance, the trees were dropping down as they rose. Alex felt the nose of the chopper dip as they picked up speed. He looked down and she was handing him the large printout. He unfolded it to see a map of what Alex judged to be a medium-size train station—nothing on the level of Geneva's or Rome's, but much bigger than a neighborhood station.

"This is Zimeysa Station!" Armstrong pointed. "It's the last major stop. There will be a lot to watch. Four platforms. Six tracks. There are arrivals and departures every fifteen minutes. He's gonna stop tonight, on the way to Geneva. *Every train does.*"

"I don't get it!" Alex yelled, studying the map. "You expect him to hop off and grab a Snickers bar?"

"He's not gonna hop off," Sangster said, next to him. "We're gonna follow *your* lead. You're going to need to check every train that goes in or out."

"The window of opportunity is eight thirty to eleven thirty," Armstrong said.

"I don't know—I don't know if I can do this," Alex confessed. "I've never tried anything like this."

"Alex, this is the closest we've ever been to being able to catch one of these guys before they get to Demon Central," Sangster said, referring to the Scholomance. "And we know he's planning something. The closest.

You are the closest. So I don't want to hear, 'I don't know' or 'what if whatever.' I want to hear, 'I'll do this damn thing.'" Sangster locked eyes with Alex, and they were crinkling at the edges—that strange mixture of hardness and mirth.

Of course. This was what he was here for. "I'll do this damn thing," repeated Alex. Armstrong nodded.

"Here we go!" shouted the pilot from up front.

Armstrong threw back the door of the Black Hawk, and wind instantly began churning through the craft. Alex saw the cement roof of a building coming up faster and felt the chopper pitch and slow.

"Zimeysa Station," Armstrong said, gesturing down. "Let's go."

CHAPTER 9

The Zimeysa Station reminded Alex of the train station in Munich, Germany, where he and his father had once spent the night. That had been awful: The whole family had been vacationing in March, and it was very cold; and on this day Alex and his father had missed the last train out of Munich, which they were supposed to catch in order to meet up with Mom and the girls, who had moved on to a villa south of Rome. He and his dad had gone to visit the concentration camps in Dachau, a bus trip, and the Dachau bus had been late getting back.

Missing the train meant that they had to cool their heels till early in the morning, which meant walking. They visited a local university and watched some TV in the student union, moved on to watch the last round of the *Glockenspiel* in a square called Marienplatz, and then settled in at the station itself. Alex and his father had huddled together against a brick wall next to a closed postcard-and-soda kiosk, Dad's jacket thrown over them. The gaping maws at either end of the station, where trains entered and departed, let the air in, and no amount of heat lamps stopped the sensation that they were on the streets. Sleeping on tile, backs against the bare wall, the cold leached into Alex's entire body. It made socks and underwear, layers of shirts, gloves, all seem to disappear. They shivered together until seven in the morning, heading to Rome with the first train. Alex had been eight years old.

It had not occurred to him until he was ten that Dad was not without means and probably could have found them a hotel room if he had so desired. Alex actually asked his father about this—catching him as he was heading out to teach at Boston University, where they had been at that time. Dad had mumbled something about how fun it had been to relive his misspent youth, which was a terrible excuse for misspending Alex's youth as well, but then Dad had been out the door.

Of course now Alex knew that just as likely, Dad had spent many of his train-station-huddling days in the employ of the Polidorium, a fact he had decidedly failed to mention.

At any rate, even in October, the Zimeysa Station was frozen stone cold, and as Alex walked up and down the platforms, he was glad that whatever else may occur, he would not be sleeping here. He'd been trained to survive in Wyoming blizzards, but anyone who felt like doing that by choice had to be crazy.

Oh, what he could have done then with what he had now—even without his backpack, his go package, Alex's pockets were lined with useful accoutrements: Besides wooden stakes, hydraulic-powered Polibows, and grappling guns, he had nifty stuff like space blankets that folded into the size of a deck of cards and small canisters of styrene that could be lit to provide warmth. And his dad probably had as well. Madman.

Nothing, not a whisper, not a bleat of static, no reverberations in his head, nothing. The only static Alex heard as he walked along the trains came off the occasional announcements, as a chipper female voice announced in French and lovely British English each arrival and departure and change of track.

Alex stopped at a magazine rack underneath an enormous white clock at the end of the station, pretending to scan the covers. He turned around to look down the six tracks. He glanced up to a spiderweb of stairs at the far end of the terminal, which allowed passengers to travel up over the tracks and down to the central platforms. At the top of the stairs, on a sort of marble terrace, Alex saw Sangster sitting at a small table with Armstrong, sipping a coffee and reading a book. Alex went to the right and started walking down the line again, down one platform, up the next, and down. Nothing through the whole sweep, and the trains emptied out. In came the next batch.

Sangster spoke through the Bluetooth in Alex's ear. "Eastbound trains on tracks two, three, and six," he said. Alex nodded. Sangster was saying that those trains were likely to stop at Geneva next.

Alex headed for track 2. People were striding across the platforms and he bumped into a woman by mistake. He kept moving. He lingered for a moment next to the first entrance to the train, where a station official eyed him for a moment and then ignored him, taking him for just another confused kid looking for his train. Alex could count on the man to not only ask him no questions, but to be silently hoping Alex wouldn't ask for any help, either.

Alex climbed up the stairs at the end and headed down to the center platforms, passing Sangster and

Armstrong as he went. Sangster didn't even glance up at him from his coffee and his copy of *The Unbearable Lightness of Being.* As Alex began to walk along track 3 on his left, he tried to reach out, cut away all noise and distraction. Nothing. Past the first ticket master and the next. Nothing.

Then he felt a whisper, a jagged hiss in his mind. Alex looked up the platform as various patrons of the station moved back and forth. "I felt something," he said, and Armstrong responded. "Where?" he heard her say in his ear.

There was a pale man in a coat at the end of the platform, just under the terrace where Sangster and Armstrong sat. He was holding a cell phone, and now took it away from his ear, staring at its screen.

Make that *very* pale. The static hissed, but the guy was fifty feet away and so close to Armstrong and Sangster that they could spill their coffee on him.

Sangster spoke sharply. "Turn around and walk, Alex, that guy is taking your picture."

Alex swiveled and started moving, scanning the trains. "How do you know?"

"He keeps sweeping the area with his phone."

"Maybe it's him I sensed," Alex whispered.

"Just look for the train."

Alex reached the end of the station, the end where he'd begun, and turned to begin the walk down the next couple of trains.

The clock chimed and the chipper voice bellowed across the cold station: "Attention: tracks two, four, and six departing immediately."

Alex started moving faster, reaching the end of train 5. "Anything?" Sangster said in his ear, from where he sat with his coffee, far behind him.

"Is the photographer still there?"

"He's moved on; I lost him in the crowd."

There was a loud cry and at the end of the station, a pair of double doors opened. A soccer team poured in, shouting as they ran, all bare legs and green shorts, down the platform. Alex headed to the entrance to train 6's last car, trying to listen, and was nearly knocked over by two Italian soccer players, both leaping up onto the train. He pushed back, shoving through the crowd.

A teenage girl in a long coat was hanging on to one of the soccer players. She laughed as she plowed into Alex, and Alex slipped around her. The crowd had grown larger. An older athlete, also in a soccer uniform but with a wool scarf over his shoulders, was shouting to the others in Italian, "*Buona, ragazzi!* Just a few minutes!"

Something hissed and buzzed in Alex's ear, in his mind but as if outside of him. He spun around as students and soccer players smashed past.

A porter was opening up a cargo panel and unloading an enormous stack of boxes onto a rolling cart. Alex tried to make eye contact with Sangster and Armstrong, but they were blocked behind the boxes and the train.

The static increased and Alex turned to face the entrance of the station, approaching train 6's entrance. The train official at the bottom of the steps did not notice him. The hissing was growing.

"Number six," Alex said, "it's number six."

Alex peered up at the windows into the train, at sleepy faces either dozing or gazing out the window. There was a man with blond hair and a leather baseball cap glancing past him, and Alex found himself staring into the man's eyes before he realized the hissing in his mind had forced him to stop.

The blond man stared back, and something like recognition came over him. He nodded, and Alex looked in the direction of his nod.

The porter slammed shut the panel on the side of the train and now he was approaching Alex at lightning speed. Alex felt something grab his collar. He opened his mouth, and a hand was placed over it. The ticket master moved away, looking elsewhere, and Alex tried to cry out as the porter dragged him onto the train, metal stairs smacking into the back of Alex's legs as he kicked.

He watched the eyes of the porter, milky and mottled and almost translucent like all the vampires'. As the porter's hand came free, Alex spoke.

"Guys!" and that was it, because the vampire porter smashed him in the side of the head and the Bluetooth went clattering onto the deck.

They were in the little entryway to the train car and no one else was coming; Alex could see that. The train lurched and began to move, and unless someone chose this moment to open the door from the passenger compartment, the porter was free to do what he did next.

He hissed like a cobra and went for Alex's throat.

Alex felt time freeze as he took in his tiny surroundings, the closed collapsing door of the train, the sliding door into the passenger section, the other sliding door into the narrow space between the two cars. They were in an area about the size of a closet.

As the vampire lunged, Alex braced himself against the wall and kicked, hard, connecting with the vampire's chest and sending him back. He winced in pain; kicking a vampire always felt like kicking a sack of sand.

He reached into his jacket and drew his Polibow, whipping it up and aiming at the porter. He was three inches away when he fired, and the vampire burst into flame, singeing Alex's eyebrows before he fell to dust.

Alex registered and ignored the acrid smell of burnt hair filling the compartment. He looked down to find that the Bluetooth had been destroyed, too, reduced to a lump of plastic under the vampire's ashes.

We're moving. Sangster must know he was on the train. Alex looked out the window and watched the station wall slide past as the train began to pick up speed, heading toward the lake.

Fine. It was time to visit the blond man.

Alex pushed the sliding door open and stepped into the train car, scanning the passengers. Of those facing toward him he felt and observed nothing of interest. Those facing away were quiet, reading, talking on cell phones. Half of them were working on laptops, the train merely an extension of their offices.

Now Alex saw someone rise and head for the door at the end—the blond man, ponytail draped over a brown leather jacket, a brown leather cap on his head. He didn't look back as he grabbed the door and went through. Alex hurried after him.

Out the door and Alex found himself stepping into

the flimsy, enclosed connector between cars. He looked through the glass and saw the blond man—the blond *vampire*—moving all the way into the next car.

His brain started to hiss as he raced along. He stepped through, and this time the car was different, and the winds in his brain began to howl.

For a brief moment Alex took the final car in—richer, full of high leather seats and proper curtains, a first-class accommodation to be sure. That was all he had time to observe before turning his attention to the gang of vampires that now looked up at him from their card tables.

Directly in front of Alex were two vampires, large and muscular men wearing tailored suits. One had a goatee, the other appeared not to have shaved—a couple of stylish vampire thugs.

Farther back, the blond man had stopped at a table and now turned toward him, as if amused. Seated at that table was a vampire who was looking down. He was pale white but not built for speed the way every other vampire Alex had observed was. This vampire had salt-and-pepper hair that curled over his forehead, and a trimmed beard that clung to a roundish face. He wore off-white pants and a white cotton peasant shirt, flowing and comfortable. Alex couldn't see the vampire's feet, but he felt certain the man would be wearing leather loafers, no socks.

All of this in less than a second, and then one of the thugs at the front snarled. Alex raised his Polibow and shot, killing him instantly, and the other was upon him, grabbing him by the throat and slamming him back against the wall.

Alex struggled against the vampire's strength, kicking, and the Polibow fell from his hands.

Answer the questions. What's going on?

One of them has me.

What do you have?

I dropped my weapon.

What else do you have?

Alex flicked his arm, bringing his metal watch to the end of his wrist. It was made of silver and he had carved a cross into the clasp. He smacked the guard in the face, holding it there. The guard's skin sizzled and he loosened his grip.

Alex took the opportunity to twist free and became aware of the blond man grabbing a long cane and walking toward him. The blond vampire whipped the cane up and hammered it against Alex's chest, below his neck, driving Alex back. Alex grabbed the cane and twisted, unable to move the vampire but able to swerve out of the way. He reached into his coat for a stake but now the guard had him again, and was grabbing his collar and slamming him back against the seat. A puff of ash flew through the air, the remains of the guard Alex had killed. The living guard held Alex down and now opened his mouth, glistening fangs showing as his head whipped back and prepared to come forward to take out his throat.

"No, no, no," said a soft, mellifluous voice. "That's enough."

The blond man with the cane froze, as did the guard.

Alex struggled to move, and the guard let him slip slightly.

The vampire in the peasant shirt was moving down the train, almost gliding, his—yep—leather loafers barely touching the floor. He stopped at the seat where Alex was pinned. Alex wondered if he could reach his stake. It was long and wooden and laced with silver, and it would do all the damage in the world. The guard had now let go of him, but Alex suspected a sudden move would be unwise.

The peasant shirt man folded his hands before his paunch, looking like a vampiric Buddha. "You must be Alex Van Helsing."

His voice was smooth, low enough to reverberate in Alex's chest, but with a strange high tenor hidden in it.

Alex found himself saying, "Yes."

"We're going to walk now, Alex. And you're going to do something for me."

Alex felt the guard completely relax his grasp and move away, and Alex sat forward. He needed to kill this man now. He needed to reach for his stake and try.

"We're going to walk," the man said again, "and you're going to do something for me."

Alex was rising and thinking he needed to reach for—something, there was something, or maybe not. Maybe not. Maybe what he was going to do now was walk.

"Let's walk."

They began to move down the car, toward the back, past the man's card table. Alex was trying to think of what it was he was going to do, just now, and in the distance he heard the vampire in the peasant shirt say to the others, "One of us will be right back."

CHAPTER 10

The train track spewed from the back of the train, red-brown and blurred, as Alex and the gray-bearded vampire stood outside in the cold and the wind. They were up against an iron railing and Alex was listening to the man talk and watching the long line of iron, watching the white gravel of the train track that melted with speed into a milky gray railroad, the dark, gray-blue evening sky stretching all around them, blanketing behind trees and ugly buildings, the view behind the view, the view no one looks at on a train.

"The truth, Alex, and we both know it, is that this is as good as it gets," said the man. His voice was audible over the wind, close behind Alex, mixing with the wind. He didn't need to shout; Alex was listening. "Relax."

Alex put his hands on the rails, watching the liquid stream of iron and gravel, listening to the liquid words.

"Your father is very proud of you, Alex, because of what you have become. Everyone who has ever known you, all those people who secretly doubted you would amount to anything, because we all know that secretly they doubted you, whatever they may have said, now even they have heard of your skills and are proud of you. Everyone is satisfied. Your mother—whose talents were so great that she could move your father to turn his back on his life—even she is amazed. All of us on the brighter side, we too are amazed. You have surprised us all. This truly is as good as it's ever going to get."

Alex nodded. All of this made sense. He understood that people generally lied when they pretended to be proud of you, but he had been doing amazing things lately. "But I thought they didn't know—"

"Of course they know," the man said. "Of course your father knows. Do you think the greatest enemy of the brighter side is stupid? We don't think that, even though it would be of great comfort to us. And, Alex, it takes *extraordinary* effort not to believe that which is of great comfort."

The man leaned closer, and Alex could hear all the crosscurrents of high and low in his voice. "Let me tell you what comforts you must not believe, Alex. You're not going to get much farther. Your friends, whatever friends you have made, will not survive being close to you. Your family will not remain proud, because of the damage you will cause. And in the end you will not be able to overcome the inherent flaws; your intellect will sadly not reach above the rather rudimentary heights it has attained now. You also, despite what you believe, will not be very tall."

Alex felt a stab of sadness at that last one, but it was just one more thing. All of this truth was exactly as he had expected.

The vampire clicked his tongue. "But look—you were able to stop a great clan lord and command the respect of a very stubborn organization. You have attained achievements most men your age could only dream of. It truly does not get any better than this."

He pointed. "The iron there is extremely spiky and hard. If you were to leap upon it, in all likelihood you would, almost instantly, be able to seal your life, seal it, here, at its best point, when you have all those things that, really, you know you only barely deserve—friends, respect, and accomplishment. And it's so easy—to step. Isn't it?"

Alex was watching the iron line and listening, and all of this made sense. There was something in the back of his mind that he had intended to do, but what the man had said made sense.

The man was talking again, like a refrain in a song, and it was true. Alex lifted his foot and hung it over the side, how easy it was. Like being in the snow, letting it close in and envelop you.

This feeling had happened once before.

Alex had been in the snow for too long the last time he had felt it, after rescuing a man on the mountain who had taken a wrong turn; Alex was a hero and then suddenly he himself had gotten lost when the rescue helicopter set off half the mountain in an avalanche. Alex had hunkered against a tree as the snow came down around him like a wave. And for what seemed like hours he had waited, so easy to go to sleep, to let the snow overtake him; he was a hero and it would never—

Alex.

He could sleep, he could step, and it would never—

Alex!

It would never be better, never to disappoint, never to overlook or outgrow, let go, step—

Beyond the droning of the voice, beyond the flowing of the rails, there was a rattling sound, a whooping sound. Something deep within him reached out for this new sound, just as he had when he had been lost in the snow. He had seen hands furiously digging toward him, digging like the coming noise, moving snow out of the way, a voice calling to him—

Alex!!

And now there was a helicopter swooping into view from over the trees, coming into view the way a pair of hands had come into view, hands reaching through the snow for him, his sister's gloves—

Take my hand!

Rattling, whooping sound of a helicopter, diving closer, thirty yards above, and Alex was reaching into his pocket. His foot still hung over the edge, and he wrapped his fingers around the handle of the palm-size grappling gun in his jacket and raised it—

Take my hand, Alex!

And fired it.

The hook looped around the skids of the chopper and Alex felt himself yank free, his shoulder twisting and screaming in pain, yes, *Wake up, take my hand, come on.*

He was swinging wildly in the air and then there were people dragging him up into the chopper, and he could barely hear Sangster and Armstrong. Alex lay on the floor of the chopper and watched the train disappear into a tunnel, as the vampire in the peasant shirt turned slowly and stepped inside.

Chapter 11

"I would have done anything he told me," said Alex, putting down his pen and bringing everyone's work to a halt. It was the next day, Tuesday. The first Pumpkin Show was that evening, and the ball in three days' time. He, Paul, Minhi, and Sid sat at an enormous round table in the New Aubrey House study, working on homework and stories for the Pumpkin Show.

Sid was writing furiously, a stack of books in front of him, opened and laid across one another as he consulted each and scribbled away on long yellow legal pads. "*The Skein* says you should use recurrent phrases to drive the reader along," he said as he wrote. "*The Skein* says if you introduce a gun on the first page you have to use it before the end."

Paul asked, "Does *The Skein* recommend you measure twice and cut once?"

Minhi offered, "Does *The Skein* recommend you not let anyone else get any work done?"

But for Sid, the ideas were flowing. Alex himself hadn't managed to get anything down. He turned instead to studying, and finally he had spoken up, haunted by the events of the night before.

Minhi laid down her own book and sighed, as though relieved that he wanted to talk about it. Alex had given them a brief run-down and then asked them to drop it. But now he found he just couldn't not talk. That was unusual for him. It was true, though: He would have done anything the vampire—Ultravox, of course—had suggested.

"You say that now," Minhi observed, "but you didn't, did you?"

Ultravox and his retinue had disappeared, either in the tunnel or somewhere along the track. The only positive side to Alex's excursion had been that Alex had seen him, and even now his description was being studied by the guys with the computers. But it was a good bet that Ultravox was at this point safely inside the protective walls of the Scholomance.

"Do you think it's true?" Paul asked, getting back to something that was bugging Alex even more than the fact that he had been about to throw himself off a moving train. "That your dad knows everything you've been up to?"

"Obviously it's not a perfect secret," Alex said. "It's hardly a secret at all. There are Polidorium people who know, there're all of you—"

"Like we're gonna be calling your mom and dad," Sid said, and snorted.

"There's my sister, and of course there's the fact that my dad isn't an idiot. He was a part of the organization."

"May I . . . ," Vienna spoke, as if unsure whether to go on.

"What's that?" Alex said.

"This is none of my business," she demurred.

"Seriously, that never stops these guys." Alex smiled. "Hey, you're the one who got sideswiped by Punk Elle. Go ahead, tell me what you're thinking."

"This man, Ultravox, he told you things in order to get you to do what he wanted," Vienna said. "My father is a negotiator and I know what such a man is like. That treaty he's working on? I've seen him talk people into supporting it even though they were dead set against it. Changing people's minds is not about bending them to your will. It's about getting them to bend their own will. What I mean is, the fact that what Ultravox said made you want to do things does not make what he said true. It just makes it something you could believe. In fact, the best lies always sound like truth. So—you really can't count on *any* of it being true."

Alex looked at Sid and Paul with a pursed frown. *Not bad.*

"Mate," said Paul, "you would do well to talk to your parents."

"*Really* talk to them," emphasized Minhi.

"I will," Alex said.

"Really?" she said, laughing.

"I think so."

"Hang on," Sid said, thinking of something else. Alex watched the boy seem to scan invisible letters hanging before him in the air. As if possessed, Sid opened up *The Skein*, ran a finger down a page, and then shut it again. Sid wrote down a few words and said, "Okay."

Paul asked, "Okay, so you're with us again?"

"Yeah," Sid said. "I think I'm good to go with the first story."

"Already?" Alex asked. "That's amazing."

"I wouldn't say amazing." Sid sat back, looking pleased. "For years I've been doing character descriptions. Now that I've learned to put a story around them, it's—well, I think I followed the advice pretty well."

"I'm not surprised—he could tell a vampire story in his sleep," Minhi said.

"Oh, my story isn't about vampires," said Sid, shaking his head. "Sorry to disappoint."

Minhi looked shocked. "Why not? That's like your subject."

"I think maybe it's too close," Sid said. "Anyway . . . I'm not sure I'm looking forward to the reading part."

"When's the first Pumpkin Show again?" Alex asked.

"Tonight," Minhi said. "It's not too late to sign up."

Chapter 12

On the way to the first Pumpkin Show, the gang passed Sangster in the lobby. He was standing near a ladder chatting with a couple of other teachers who were watching a pair of older boys hang a chandelier. They were surrounded by wires and cables and for a moment Alex had the vision of the boys on the ladder being eaten alive by the wiring, sucked up through the ceiling. He needed to stop listening to Sid.

Alex dropped back from his friends as Sangster glanced at Alex and excused himself. It was obvious to Alex that Sangster had been waiting for him. "Let's walk," Sangster said.

They went down the hall, past rooms that were still full of cobwebs and sheets and even, strangely, a pair of genuine giant-wheeled bicycles like the one that Alex and his mom had seen Paul Newman ride in *Butch Cassidy and the Sundance Kid.* They exited out the side, and as they began to walk the long way, hugging the mossy wall of the grounds, he could see that Sangster had something serious to tell him.

"What?" Alex asked.

"Armstrong passed along some more Chatterbox intel on Scholomance," Sangster answered. "A reprimand went through for your friend Elle. She's angry as hell, because a project she was working on is being canceled. Project Claire, it's called."

"Claire," Alex said. In his mind he instantly saw a skeleton, female, long hair barely visible underneath a white veil. The skeleton was alive, but barely, and had been drinking the blood of the Clan Lord Icemaker. Icemaker had nearly gotten *Alex's* blood in order to revive her completely, so that Icemaker and Claire could rule together. But, thanks to Alex, it hadn't worked out.

Sangster said, "We did wonder what happened to Claire. Now we know; Claire the skeleton has been sitting at the Scholomance, and Elle has been leading the project to finish bringing her to life, and the bosses just pulled the plug."

Alex shrugged. "I guess I don't get why this is a big deal."

"It's just information you might be able to use against a vampire who seems very interested in taking you apart," Sangster said. "Anyway, their chief frustration with Elle is that she failed to kill you. She was supposed to tear out your throat or something and instead she got all clever with the Glimmerhook worm. But look, they're calling you by *name*. They wanted *you* out of the way before Ultravox got here." Sangster looked around.

Alex thought of the train. "But if I was supposed to be out of the way for Ultravox—Sangster, that guy could have just pushed me off that train himself."

"I have a theory about that," Sangster whispered. "Ultravox likes to do things his way. Before we lost the chatter lines we were following, you know what the vampires were saying? That as upset as the Scholomance was, Ultravox was simply *amused*. But, Alex, I think he wants to know whether in fact you are a threat. I think he's testing you."

"Testing me how?"

"There's something special about you, and it has them worried." Sangster tapped his head. "We don't really know much about this thing you have up here. Your ancestor Abraham may have had it, and we think his first son did, too. But not everyone has it. Your father didn't."

"But he managed," Alex said.

Sangster said, "Oh, yeah, he managed. But you do have it. First in a couple generations as far as we can tell. So far *you* use it to sense them. Maybe there's more to it. But—that might be beyond the Polidorium's ability to help with. I have to say it's getting dangerous," Sangster said. "Not one of us would think any less of you if you decided to leave."

Alex sighed. *Getting* dangerous? For a moment he shot through the whole scenario—leaving the Polidorium, leaving Glenarvon, going home, and then what? School in the U.S.? Take up woodworking? "I'm not leaving unless you kick me out," he said.

"Okay, partner," Sangster said. Alex had absolutely no idea if Sangster was relieved or not, and he didn't trust the casual language to be any indication of Sangster's feelings at all. He was the most unreadable person Alex had ever met. "So that's it. Ultravox is in Geneva; he's here to do something, and we don't know what it is. We have a lot of work to do."

But first, the opening Pumpkin Show.

The LaLaurie library was dimly lit, and Alex realized with some regret that this was his first time seeing it. It spilled out before him with high stacks and catwalks going up three stories, and he could make out the green reading lamps you expected to find at an Ivy League university rather than a high school. "This is cool," Alex said to himself, pushing past a crowd of students to stand inside the entrance.

There Alex found Sid, who looked as pale as a ghost, surrounded by Paul, Minhi, and Vienna. Sid had drawn the third slot and was flipping through his papers nervously.

"When do they begin?" Alex asked Minhi. He looked at the place of honor that had been set: a large chair that almost qualified as a throne, surrounded by candles, with a reading table placed in front of it.

"Ms. Daughtry will start us off," Minhi said.

"Everybody, welcome," came the voice of Ms. Daughtry, emerging from the back of the library as if on cue. She went straight to the candles, talking as she went. "I don't know how many of you are familiar with our ritual, so I'll set the stage, and then we'll be off. Please, by all means, take a seat."

After the gathered students found chairs and tables to lean on or stand against, Daughtry continued.

"The Pumpkin Show is a LaLaurie tradition that dates back to our founding. For decades it was exclusively for reading original stories, though in recent years we've expanded the competition to include artistic works of any kind. We take as our inspiration the salons of antiquity, before the age of the Xbox and the internet, when our only defense against the cold and damp was one another. The most famous model comes from just up the lake," she said.

"At the Villa Diodati," whispered Alex as Daughtry said the words aloud. He knew the place well.

"It was here on Lake Geneva in 1816 that Europe's greatest living writer, Lord Byron, gathered with a small retinue of friends, including Percy and Mary Shelley, and shared stories—and not just any stories, but ghost stories and other tales of the supernatural. It was not without its success. The results of that story circle include some of English literature's most enduring works: Shelley's *Frankenstein*, Byron's *Fragment*, and John Polidori's *Vampyre*."

Alex's head swam with rivers of meaning behind each of these little markers of Geneva history. The lake was alive with connections to the Diodati circle. *Frankenstein* had held coded warnings about the return of Byron in the guise of a powerful vampire clan lord. Polidori, the minor name in the bunch, had been the master of a clue hidden in Shelley's book, and had founded the organization that had so taken over Alex's life. And yet here that cast of characters was, back in their place as the backdrop to a story contest. Which seemed just.

"So. The first reader will take his or her place at the seat of honor and, as we say, *declaim*." There was a chuckle. "And you'll want to shout that, by the way. Our young authors often like to start their readings by giving us a lot of apologies about whether their story is any good. 'I've just started on this,' 'This is a first draft,' 'I don't know what I was thinking.'" She smiled. "That's when to shout. So, without further ado—Minhi Krishnaswami?"

Paul squeezed Minhi's shoulder and she headed up to the seat. Minhi took a moment to adjust herself in the large, reddish chair, and shuffled her papers a bit. "Mine is called 'The Ice,'" she said. "And I'm really sorry, but it's still in the—"

"*Declaim!*" came a bunch of female voices, and Minhi began.

"The Ice." Alex expected, when he heard that title, that Minhi was going to raid her own experience at the hands of the Icemaker, of being dragged across a frozen lake and down to the Scholomance underneath. He had been surprised that she would be so daring, to tell a story of her own horror. But he was relieved to be wrong. "The Ice" was a tale of a ship trapped in a glacier. Thoroughly horrifying—there were deaths by freezing and heroic attempts to get away, and a final surrender to cold death—but it was a horror of imagination and not of confession. People listened, rapt, as she read in that elegant voice of hers, the slight Indian accent and American phrasings. This was the second time Alex had watched her perform, and it was clear she loved and commanded the spotlight. Previously he had seen her performing *Hung Gar* kung fu, and that, too, was entrancing.

When she was done she received her applause with a mix of pleasure and slight, charmingly perfect humility, and then the seat was taken by another student Alex didn't know.

Sid was third of the evening, and Alex watched his friend slowly move to the front and take his seat. The thin boy with ginger hair squirmed a bit as he gathered his papers. He opened his mouth, looking like he was about to pass out. Alex wanted to shout in support but let it go.

"'The Box.'"

Sid began to read, his voice quavering at first and then slowly building into a confident sound that never gave out for all fifteen pages of his manuscript. As Sid read, Alex heard all the things Sid had learned. He heard cadence and rhythm and repeating mantralike phrases.

Sid even pulled out what sounded to Alex like a high-wire act of words, in which he managed to end every short scene with sentences that echoed one another without repeating. Alex had the suspicion that he was even missing half the tricks. Somehow, Sid had become a master of composition. The difference between what Sid was doing with words and what Alex himself could do—based on what he churned out in English assignments, anyway—was like the difference between an Olympic ice dancer and a Sunday ice-skater. The tools were the same but the result was orbiting on a higher plane.

The story was of ghosts in a tower, of hidden messages in a silver box, all right, but beyond that it was a presentation of foreboding. It built on itself, tightening the screws of suspense and then releasing, tightening and releasing, and at the end snapping in a crescendo of shock and tragedy.

Alex watched the crowd. The students, especially the girls, were not merely engaged; they were held tight to their seats and transfixed.

There was a chestnut-haired Asian girl, tall enough that Alex guessed she was a senior, standing along the wall. Alex watched her sway slightly as she listened. Another girl, blond and wearing a lavender sweater, had gone glassy at the eyes, her mouth slightly parted.

Alex was awed by the power of Sid's reading. In his years of making characters, Sid had become a master of story, and his audience was held in his hypnotic sway. When he was done, there was an electric silence. It took Ms. Daughtry, who began clapping, to rip the silence open into a shock of applause.

Alex had no idea a story could do that to its listeners. In that instant he was insanely proud of his friend. For one person at least, the move to LaLaurie had netted a clear triumph.

There were other stories in the evening, but Minhi and Sid had put themselves in the minority by choosing prose: Alex and Paul endured a litany of pop songs, monologues from *The Crucible*, *Rosencrantz and Guildenstern Are Dead*, and *The Children's Hour*, an authentic yodeling demonstration from a German girl, and one poem by Maya Angelou. Alex found himself wishing Minhi had done her *Hung Gar*, or at least used it on the yodeling girl.

After the readings were over, Ms. Daughtry made a few announcements about the next heats: This was Round One. There were two more to go. Ten contestants would make it, no telling who, but one of them was in no doubt. Sid had been the master, and that had ended the evening well before its actual finale.

Chapter 13

Visiting Steven at Secheron Hospital on Wednesday was a nuisance that none of them had time for, but they did it anyway. The second Pumpkin Show was that night and the ball—just two days away—was occupying the girls' every thought. (Alex had yet to ask Sid how the first rehearsal went.) Alex had almost begged off from the hospital visit except that Minhi had insisted that it would mean a lot to Vienna and somehow that was that. Alex felt overwhelmed by demand.

Everything not destroyed in the fire had been moved to LaLaurie, and Alex rode the spare bicycle he habitually borrowed from Sid—he kept forgetting that he needed to ask his parents to ship him one. They pedaled all the way into town.

Going into town required a bike or a bus. It was nicer by bike, Paul had told him, and this was still true even now that they had about twice as far to go, around the lake and into Secheron Village. As they rode, Alex was watching the trees, half expecting Elle to appear.

They clustered near one another on the road, and Minhi asked something that Alex had a hard time keeping straight himself. "Sid, how does someone become a vampire, anyway?"

"There are a lot of different stories," said Sid. "But the one that seems to be true is that it's a curse and a poison both. You get the poison and it can kill you. If you die from it and you haven't been embalmed or cremated already, you rise again. But there are lots of halfway points. You can be a *thrall*."

"A what?"

"A thrall, you know, a servant. Sometimes those are just people who really love vampires," Sid explained. "And sometimes they're people who have been bitten, who already are poisoned, who are on the way themselves."

"I'm glad you're finally finding a use for all this info," Minhi said.

"Tell you what *I* wish," Alex said. "Sometimes I wish

I could just download your brain into mine."

Alex was relieved to put away thoughts of vampires when they locked their bikes at the hospital and headed in to visit Steven Merrill.

Unlike the tony, new feel of the village library and marina, the hospital was bland and utilitarian and looked as though it had been built in the mid-sixties, with sweeping, ugly arcs and thin modern columns. Awful architecture was a mainstay the world over.

As Vienna signed the papers at the front desk Alex looked at Paul and Sid.

"Can you believe we're doing this?" he muttered.

Paul shrugged. "Seems like the right thing to do."

Minhi had been asking directions from the nurse behind the desk and now returned to them. "Elevator's out," she said. "Third floor."

They were used to stairs. Alex shivered at the colossal dreariness of the place. A flash of color caught his eye as they neared the stairs, reflections of gold paper. He peered in the trash can with curiosity as he passed. It was a box of chocolates, crushed and dumped, next to the plainer paper it had been shipped in. The label said MERRILL. Alex filed it away—Bill was in a bad mood, so trashing a care package was within the realm of irrational things he might do.

As they walked up the white plaster stairwell—Alex could never understand why anyone painted stairs white when it made them look dingier than they could possibly actually be—Alex turned to Sid and Vienna. "I didn't even ask how rehearsal went Monday night."

Sid shook his head. "I think I'm no Steven Merrill."

"Sid did very well," Vienna said. They reached the third floor. "I think after a few more times he would be perfect."

Alex was cursing himself slightly. Rehearsing for the ball certainly would have been better than the train ordeal. Plus he was now well on the way to putting Sid next to Vienna for the rest of the week. Because this clever strategy of putting his friends close to any girl he found remotely interesting was working out so well already.

Vienna pushed through the door and Sid turned to him. "Dude, you gotta take my place."

"Really?" Alex said.

"Yes, really," Paul whispered. "Sid nearly fell down the stairs."

"I thought the *debutantes* come down the stairs—"

"Seriously, you gotta take my place," Sid said, his face crinkled.

Vienna held the door open and said, "You know I'm

standing right here, right?" She looked at Minhi as they all stepped into the third-floor hall.

Alex paused for a beat. Okay, sure. "So . . . would you mind terribly if I took Sid's place?"

"I think we can make that work," Vienna said, with only a Mona Lisa smile in evidence.

Abruptly Vienna stopped, and Alex felt the smile drain from his own face as he looked down the hallway. This was not a huge hospital—one central hallway traveled down the floor—and on a weekday afternoon there should have been a flurry of activity. But all was silent. The only visible soul was Bill Merrill, who was leaning with his hands thrust into his sport coat against the wall next to a hospital room door.

Vienna spoke first. "Bill?"

Bill seemed to come awake, heaving himself off the wall as he looked up toward them. Alex saw what seemed to be wistfulness dry up and dissolve into something angrier. "What are you doing here?" Bill demanded. As he came closer, he pointed at Alex. "What is *he* doing here?"

Bill was not at all himself. The Bill that Alex knew would immediately attack him—naturally—but he would have smiled while doing it or seemed bored and halfhearted. Bill now was agitated and forceful, and intent on pushing them back without saying it; his hands were up and faced toward them as though he were blocking access to the VIP section of a nice restaurant.

"He's here because he wanted to see how Steven is doing," Vienna said softly, as though talking to a child.

"We came to visit," said Alex.

"Shut up," Bill said as soon as Alex opened his mouth. "Shut up!"

"Why aren't you in the room?" Vienna asked.

Minhi started moving down the hall and the other four followed, pushing past Bill without touching him, and Bill started backing up.

"Wait—" Bill said. Alex's head filled with static. Alex looked sideways at Paul who held up his hands, as if agreeing with Bill. Alex headed for the door. Bill stepped in his way.

"What's going on, Bill?" Alex said, and he felt his voice betraying the alarm going off in his head.

"Now's a bad time," Bill said. "Even you can understand that. Go back. Vienna, it's a bad time. Get out." Bill pointed at each of them, Alex, Sid, Paul, and Minhi. "Take *him* back, take *him* back, take *him* back, and take *her* back and GET THE HELL OUT."

Alex watched Bill's eyes—then ran for the room. He stopped in the doorway, looking through to see a doctor with his back to him, brown hair and a sterile blue cap on his head, blue scrubs at the shoulders. Then the doctor stepped away.

Alex now saw a room of four people dressed in scrubs and moving around the bed. Steven's legs were covered in blankets. Two of the doctors were setting up a gurney next to the bed.

Behind them, crumpled in the corner, lay a man in blue scrubs with a stream of red flowing liberally down from his throat.

Alex started to turn when Bill grabbed him by the shoulder, spinning him around and then socking him in the face. Alex's vision went thoroughly gaga for a second until he snapped back as Bill slammed him against the wall, his fingers around his collar.

"What are you doing?" Alex whispered to Bill, stunned. "Don't you know what they are?"

Alex twisted away and ran for Steven's door.

Bill grabbed him and dragged him. "Get out, get out, haven't you done enough?" he shrieked.

Out of nowhere, Minhi stepped between them with her fists linked together, slamming her forearms down on Bill's arm. Bill dropped Alex.

Two people in scrubs came out guiding a gurney with a white sheet over the form in it, followed by two more people. Alex could see Steven's face at one end of the gurney, pale and waxy—but dead? It was impossible to tell. "They're taking him!" Alex shouted.

Paul and Sid came running alongside Alex. One of the doctors with a blue cap over her head looked back, and Alex recognized Elle's eyes in an instant. She started running with the gurney toward the elevator while the other three "doctors" squared off, blocking the boys' path.

Alex, Sid, and Paul stopped as Minhi came up next to them, halting as well. The three vampires stood perfectly still. They folded their arms, three blue guards.

Alex spoke over his shoulder to Bill, who was behind him, near Vienna. "You can't do this, Bill, you can't let them take him. You have no idea what you're getting into."

"They're not taking him," Bill said, coming up and passing Alex, stepping through the line of doctors. The elevator chimed—hmm, so it wasn't busted after all—and Elle pushed the gurney on. Bill got on the elevator as well. "They're taking us."

Alex said urgently, "Bill, they'll kill him."

Bill shook his head, and Alex wasn't sure if Bill meant to say that Alex was wrong, or that Steven was dead already.

"Bill, stop!" Vienna cried, running now down the hallway toward Bill.

"I can't believe you would bring him here," Bill said to her, referring to Alex with scorn. "I thought you were our friend."

One of the doctor-vampires grabbed Vienna, stopping her progress. Minhi sprang into action. *Hung Gar* kung fu always delivered powerful blows that could, in Sangster's terms, "take your head off."

Minhi jumped, bringing her leg up and down, coiling and uncoiling straight into the knee of the vampire on the right, who had grabbed Vienna. The knee folded back with a solid crunch and the vampire howled in anger, dropping Vienna and turning his attention to Minhi.

Alex reached for the stake hidden in his jacket and raised it, plunging it into the chest of the wounded vampire. An explosion of dust hit the air. The doors of the elevator closed.

Now the other two vampires broke off their guard duty, hurtling through the door into Steven's room.

Alex heard a burst of reinforced glass and they looked to see Steven's window busted out, cheap aluminum blinds swinging in the wind.

"Come on," Alex said. They raced for the stairs.

Less than a minute to reach the lobby, and another few seconds to the front entrance.

But they were too late. In the front bay, an ambulance was already pulling away, a plain white van that roared and sped into the distance. In its back window Alex saw Bill, staring.

"Just get back here" was all Sangster had to say on the phone as they pedaled furiously from the village. Alex could barely look at the others, until finally he burst out with, "Is this my fault?"

"What?" Minhi asked, next to him.

"I can't—Steven was injured because of me—Minhi, the Scholomance just took the Merrill brothers. Not just Steven but both of them."

"That was *not* the same as when Paul and I were taken," Minhi said. He looked at her face and saw that she wasn't trying to go easy on him. She shook her head defiantly. "You saw Bill. He was helping them."

"Why would he do that?"

"Because," Sid said darkly, "he was headed that way. Don't you think?"

"You think just because he was a jerk he was waiting for the right moment to become a vampire?" Alex spat out the words, distraught. "It can't work that way. We all know jerks, Sid. I know how to deal with the Merrills; I have a sister just like them back home. A *twin*."

Sid had no response to that.

Vienna pulled ahead of them. "All of you, stop. You don't know them."

"You tell us, then," Alex said. "From what we know of the vampires, they offer a—it's a powerful life, or after-life. But it lacks all the things that make us what we are. Elle told us the process, whatever it is, burns out whatever empathy, whatever love you have left. So you tell us: Do you think that's something the Merrills would sign up for?"

"Years ago I would have said no," said Vienna. "But they've changed."

Alex swore inwardly. So much to clean up; there was a dead doctor back there and they were racing away without talking to a soul.

When they reached LaLaurie, it was getting dark. Alex saw Sangster waiting on the front steps as they chained up their bikes and he immediately broke ahead of his friends. "You've got to do whatever you can," he said to Sangster, approaching the steps at a trot.

"Alex—"

"We found our way into the Scholomance once before, we can step it up again," Alex said. "There's no way they know what they're getting into. We can do it tonight."

"Alex!" Sangster said again.

"*What?*" Alex shot back, and then he heard a second voice.

"Alex."

Alex turned around. Waiting patiently in the foyer next to a framed LaLaurie crest were two Americans: the woman blond and trim in a cashmere wrap, the man goateed, with dark wavy hair and a midnight blue topcoat.

"Mom? Dad?"

Chapter 14

They weren't the only parents. As Alex accompanied them to a place where they could talk in private, he noticed other adults throughout the school. It had been bound to happen. The parents were descending on LaLaurie and the Kingdom of Cots, and they wanted answers.

As he walked up the stairs Alex turned to them and said, "I'd show you my room, but—"

"No, no, apparently it burned up," said his mother. "We were talking to your Mr. Sangster about it."

Silence after that until Alex found a chemistry lab upstairs and shut the door. Like all such spaces it looked like a junior mad scientist's lab, Bunsen burners and microscopes under leatherette coverlets. The room was lined with glass windows, half of which were open even in the fall, ready to vent noxious fumes. Outside, he could see the tree-lined parking lot and many rented vehicles. He dragged a couple of chairs from behind the first row of black countertops.

The three of them stared at the chairs.

"Oh, Alex," Mom said, and then she hugged him again. She held him out, surveying him. "My God, you look gaunt."

"He always looks gaunt," said Dad.

"Sorry, I guess," said Alex. He ran his fingers through his hair. Where to start? There wasn't time for this now. "Look, I—I wish I could spend more time, but there's an emergency."

"I should say so," Mom said. "Alex, what are you thinking? Your school is *destroyed*, you're at an entirely new place, and you can't see fit to fill us in?"

"I know, that's really . . . terrible, but I mean, right now I need to follow up on something." What was he going to say? He looked at his father, and a million things raced through his mind. *Your father knows. The greatest enemy knows. Your mother is proud of you.* Was any of that true? Now it felt like a dream. But at this moment, right this instant, there were two students who had just been lost to the Scholomance, and he had no idea how much his father actually knew, no idea what his mother knew, and no time. "There's a rehearsal I'm supposed to be in," he said, remembering that he had agreed to take Sid's place for the ball.

"We brought you some clothes, some new glasses, some school supplies. That nice Mr. Sangster had someone take them to your dormitory," Mom said. "But we have to make some decisions. Your sister was very worried about you."

"What did—" Alex tried to look down the chessboard and choose his words like moves. *What did she tell you* wouldn't do. "I mean, I want to— Where are you staying? We could have breakfast."

Alex touched her sleeve. Instantly he felt the warmth of her, the safety of her presence. His mother and father had raised him to look after himself and his sisters. It was a house, he had thought, of adventure and honesty. But that was before he had learned of all the secrets his father harbored. And so far his father hadn't really said a word.

"I gotta hurry," Alex said, walking toward the door. "I'll bet there's some kind of reception for you guys; there has to be."

"We have to decide, Alex," Mom said.

"I don't know what that means, but I'm sure we can decide over breakfast." He reached for the door and pulled it open.

There was a whisper, words he didn't understand, and the door was pulled from his hands and slammed shut. A crackle of energy shot through the room, fizzing his hair as the lights flickered. Alex froze as every window slapped closed at once. He slowly turned as the wind from the closing windows lifted the coverlets and sent papers shuffling.

His parents stood side by side. His mom's long hair was floating slightly off her coat.

His father was the one who spoke this time.

"We have to decide if you're going to stay with the Polidorium."

CHAPTER 15

Alex stared in shock. "Holy—what the heck was that?" He looked at the windows and the papers still settling around the room. "Oh my God, *who are you*?"

The being that surely did look like his mother rolled her eyes, adjusting her wrap. "Alex, settle down, I'm your mother."

"Oh, no!" Alex exclaimed. "No, no, *Mom*, I've known you my whole life and you've never slammed a door with your *mind*, and we slam a *lot* of doors."

"I didn't slam it with my mind," she said simply, taking a seat.

"I just watched you; one minute I'm leaving and the next minute you're going all *Carrie* with the doors and the windows."

Dad scoffed lightly, smiling some. "She did it with a spell."

"A *spell*?" This was too much. Alex ran his fingers through his hair again, pacing. "Since when, I mean—I mean, we don't *do* these things. These things *don't happen*! When did you start using spells?"

"When I was about your age, actually," she said.

In the back of his mind, a snippet of a conversation played, something Director Carreras had said: *We all know about Amanda.*

What does that mean?

It means that if not for your mother, your father would probably still be with the Polidorium, Sangster had said. But Carreras had meant more than that, hadn't he?

"Back up, back up, back up," Alex said.

"Do you want to sit?" his mother said, indicating a chair.

"No." He frowned.

His father spun the empty chair around and sat down, resting his arms on the seat back.

Alex turned to his dad. "I mean, what—what was all that growing up about *this doesn't happen*. 'Oh, that thing you just saw in a movie, no, that doesn't happen. Van Helsing name? Coincidence.' "

"I'm sorry, Alex. It seemed like the right way to go about it all."

"Dad! Mom! I don't know if you know, but there are vampires out here. Actual vampires with, you know, fangs. There's this one with punky hair and crazy eyes and I can't seem to lose her. These people want my hide. There're no *spells*, though, that's an all-new little surprise!"

"Witches are actually fairly rare," Dad said.

"And now you're all professorly about the witch-to-vampire ratio, *Dad*! When were you going to let me in on this?"

The three of them looked at one another. His mother's arms were crossed, and she looked a bit defensive, his father with his fingers laced together, gazing down. He couldn't hide that he seemed to think this was funny. Finally his father said, "We discussed it on the plane and honestly, we came to the conclusion that you probably knew most of it by now."

"That's not—that doesn't even come close to—that's just about whether you were going to talk about it, when were you going to *tell* me?"

"You know how when you're little and you believe in Santa Claus? We need some fresh air," his mother interrupted herself. She whispered something in a language he didn't recognize, and one of the windows slid open. She looked back at him, flipping her hair out of the way.

"Anyway, it's always nicer if the kids find out first by themselves."

"Yeah!" Dad agreed. "They see you taking down the presents, and then they *help*."

"This isn't Santa Claus," Alex spat. "Santa Claus turns out not to be real. The vampires went the *other way*." He sighed, shaking his head, and breathed slowly. "When I got kicked out of Frayling, the boy I fought with was—"

"A werewolf," Dad said. "And we talked about telling you then, but we thought we could give you a few more years of, you know, *innocence* might be the word."

"Did you know that the Polidorium was here at Lake Geneva?"

"Well, I know they're everywhere, but no, I did not know that they had a large base here. And I *also* didn't expect that you would wind up working with them."

"They gave him a motorcycle," his mom said, clucking in disapproval.

"I didn't expect that either."

"I don't understand," Alex said, "I mean, any of it, but right now I don't understand what you know. How much—what do you—?"

"What do we know about your activities here?" Mom asked.

"Right, that's a start. We'll trade information."

"I would advise you not to do that unless we ask," his father said rapidly. Ever the company man.

"It started with a vision," Mom said, "during a meditation session. It was a vision of a powerful witch, angry with you, but weak, unable to stop you."

"I haven't met any witches," Alex said again. "Do you mean someone at the Scholomance?"

Mom shrugged.

Alex asked, "What else did you see?"

"That vision was not mine," said Mom. "It was—someone I was meditating with."

"Uh, okay," Alex said. Briefly he wondered who the other witches in his mother's life were. She belonged to roughly a dozen charitable boards—was there a coven among them?

"And then I looked for you, spiritually looked for you—that's hard to explain. But I didn't see any danger." She looked at Dad. "But that wasn't good enough for me; I had your father do some checking up."

"After that it was easy. The Polidorium can be leaky sometimes," said Dad. "I got into some minor databases and saw some of the equipment that had been issued to you. I talked to some people I know."

"Do you know Sangster?"

"Your teacher?" Dad asked.

"Right."

"What did I tell you about *only if we ask*?"

"Okay," said Alex helplessly.

"So it seems like you've gotten involved," said Dad, "a little earlier than we'd hoped, but honestly this conversation was gonna happen sometime."

"He's fourteen years old, Charles," said Mom.

"Oh, come on, Amanda, it's Alex, he's a survivalist—we had soldiers in the Revolutionary War who were fourteen."

"You said," Alex broke in, "that we need to make a decision. So, who makes it? Would that be me, or would that be you?" He almost wanted the release of them taking charge. When he first started working with Sangster he had felt nothing but the rush of adrenaline every time he saw the Polidorium emblem, but now, with Vienna, and the Merrills, things had gotten . . . complicated.

"Is that what you want?" Mom asked, leaning forward. "Do you want us to decide for you?"

"Well . . . ," Alex said.

"Because I know what I would choose," she said intensely. "I would choose that you come home. It's not safe. It's too early to give up your life."

"There's no reason to think he's gonna give up his life." Dad scowled. "They have all the equipment, and a lot more backup than he would in Wyoming."

"And they wouldn't come *looking* for him if he hadn't gotten involved in your little *fraternity*."

"They're not wearing togas and playing beer pong, Mom," said Alex.

"How do you know about *beer pong*? Do they allow drinking at—"

Alex waved his hands. "They don't even allow video games at this school. And you know what else? The Polidorium doesn't let me use a gun. Everyone's looking out for me, okay?"

"I'm sort of surprised at that about the guns," Dad said.

"Right, because of the Revolutionary War," Alex retorted. "You know, I saw a picture of you in, like, Prague, with a gun and rubble and stuff."

"That's a pretty good description of my time there."

Alex found himself laughing. He looked at them both. What he said next had to be good. It had to sound like he had his wits about him or the discussion would be over. He took a moment, looking down the mental chessboard again, and then laid it out. "When I found out there was such a thing as the Polidorium, it was like a light went on. It was like this was what I had been looking for. I wanted in. The truth is, I didn't tell you guys because I was afraid of what this talk here could become. I didn't want you to swoop in and take me home."

"And now?" Mom asked.

"Look, I know I'm fourteen and it's not really normal for me to say there's a job to do, but it's very close to that. This is what my life is supposed to be. I can feel that. I have friends here, and I'm learning here."

Dad nodded. "Alex, I'm not a part of the Polidorium life anymore. We have five children, and two of them are still small. If this is what you want to do for now, we won't force you to come home. But I have to urge you: Use everything. Pay very close attention. Listen to your instincts. We'll be staying in Geneva tonight, and then we're out of here before dawn—we have to be in London for a trust meeting tomorrow afternoon. But look, the instant you want to give up or it gets too hot, call us."

"What your father is saying," Mom said, "is that your family has been a part of a war for a long time, but *you* don't have to be a part of it."

Dad chewed his lip. "No, no. No, he probably does. But it's up to him whether it's time."

"Now," said Mom. "We all have to go to the library, because apparently there's something called the Pumpkin Show."

CHAPTER 16

It was time for the second Pumpkin Show, but a pall lay over this one as parents filed into the library—guests impatiently waiting for their real purpose, a conference with the administration that would follow the performance.

Alex left his parents to mingle and found Minhi, Vienna, and Paul standing around some empty seats near the front. Minhi was thumbing through the program. "Sid's *last*," she said excitedly. That was a prime spot. There were only ten students competing tonight: some songs, some monologues, a dancer, and Sid's story. It was a new one; they had no idea what about. The yodeler hadn't made it, but Alex noticed her chatting with Sid near the big chair. Well, go, Sid.

Alex looked at Vienna. "Are you okay?" He meant about Steven.

She bit her lip. "I'm trying not to think about it."

The various parents looked somewhat agitated, not surprising considering most of them were here to decide whether to let their sons stay. Inviting them all to a school event probably had made sense in a decorum sort of way, but there was palpable anxiety in the air.

Sangster was looking through some papers at a table next to the bookshelves and Alex caught his eye. "You talk to any of the parents?" Alex asked, coming over.

"A few. They're not sure we're doing this transition right."

"It's been less than a week," Alex said. "What do they want?"

"Alex, it's impossible to overstate how traumatizing an event like that can be for people. Lots of parents want to pull their kids out," Sangster said. "How about yours?"

Alex shrugged. "They're letting me stay. Look, we have to talk about what happened at the hospital. There's a dead doctor. And the Scholomance was there; Elle was with them." Suddenly Alex had a thought and looked around. "Are the Merrills' parents here?"

Sangster shook his head. He seemed to consider something for a moment, then pulled out a sheet of paper. "Look at this," Sangster said as he handed it to Alex.

"Are you listening to me? We had another kidnapping," Alex said urgently.

"Just—read it," the teacher said. "And then give it back to me, because that's confidential."

Alex took the sheet of paper and studied it for a moment. It was an official form from the Glenarvon Academy office. He saw the subject line, read on, then looked up. The subject line was essentially the entire document. Alex looked around, but nobody seemed to be paying attention to them. "This is a withdrawal notice," Alex said, confused.

"For Bill and Steven Merrill," Sangster said quietly. "That's on their parents' orders. School got a message saying that Steven and Bill were going to be picked up at the hospital and not to expect them to return."

"This has to be a fake," Alex said, handing it back. "I mean, the form is real, but I just saw a bunch of vampires take them away."

"I understand," Sangster said. "But Otranto received the phone call himself."

"Anyone can make a phone call," Alex insisted. "I could do that."

"Alex," said Sangster, "did they try to get away, the Merrills? Did they ask for your help?"

"No, they . . ."—Alex had to sigh—"Bill was in charge. He wanted us gone."

"Think about it," said the teacher. "Soon they'll be just two of perhaps scores of students taken out over the next hour, if I had to guess. The Merrills are gone, and if what you tell me is correct, they made a deal we can't stop."

"You think the Merrills' parents deliberately handed them over to the Scholomance?" Alex looked around again, keeping his voice down. "I thought that organization was a secret."

"The parents in these schools are some of the most connected people in the world, in politics, business, and everything else," said Sangster. "The Merrills are part of a very old family in New York. Shuttling away children is not unheard of."

"It's the *Scholomance.* Why would they do that? What kind of parents would do such a thing?"

"Maybe they thought it was their last hope for Steven," said Sangster. "I don't know. But right now we have to stay on task. What about your parents?"

"Like I said, they're cool," Alex said, looking back at the two of them, chatting with some other parents. Dad glanced at him briefly. Dad the retired spy. Mom the—the witch.

There was a buzz of activity in the library as Mr. Otranto entered in his usual elegant topcoat, bearing a briefcase. He headed for the center of the room and took his place.

"Oh," Sangster said. "I called the hospital. The dead doctor you mentioned? There's no record of him either. And this time it's not us doing the covering up."

Alex stared. "Jeez."

"Ladies and gentlemen, thank you for coming," said Mr. Otranto. "I know we have a lot of visitors. I myself am a visitor, so it weighs heavily on me. What I hope we accomplish tonight is a beginning of a shared destiny, if you will. But first I know that you will all enjoy seeing what these young men and women have been up to. Ms. Daughtry?"

For the second night in a row, Daughtry kicked off the evening as Alex went to take a seat with Paul, Minhi, and Vienna. Paul had an empty seat next to him, and there was also an empty seat between Minhi and Vienna. For a moment Alex froze, completely thrown by this choice. *Computer, run diagnostic.* He sat between the girls.

Behind him he heard some students studying the program and whispering, "A new one, a new one." He realized they were talking about Sid's story. After one night, he had fans.

Sid's story tonight was called "The Iron Veil," and it was a creepy little tale of unrequited love and an unpleasant discovery, in a strange, dreamy world of castles and knights. It came across more like a poem than had his previous work: more repeating phrases and rhythms within rhythms. When it finally wound its way to a climax of horror, Alex became aware that he had been drawn to the edge of his seat—the literal edge of his seat!—but that was nothing compared to the effect on the other students, especially some of the girls. They were as enrapt as before, with the same glassy-eyed, forward-leaning expression. That was some mojo Sid was working, especially, Alex noted with some astonishment, with the dozen or so senior girls in the room.

Alex threw Paul a smile that suggested they should all give up right now and start taking advice from Sid from then on.

After the readings were over, Ms. Daughtry made a few announcements about the next and final round coming in a few days. And then she shooed them all away for the parents' conference.

Alex wasn't there for that, but when his parents took their leave later, to go to their hotel in Geneva, he learned that it had been the civil bloodbath that

Sangster predicted, since it appeared that returning to Glenarvon's campus was not going to be as fast as most parents had hoped. By the next morning Glenarvon Academy was seventy-five students lighter, bringing them down to one hundred, and the Merrills were just another ripple in the wave.

Chapter 17

It was one in the morning in the Kingdom of Cots, and Alex awoke suddenly to the sound of crashing glass in the distance. His eyes shot open and he was awake. For a moment he was confused about where he was, forgetting about the shrouds that hung around each bed on the riggings that had been put up, hospital style, throughout the gym.

Alex blinked, reaching for his new glasses underneath the cot and putting them on, and sat up.

The room was full of the sounds of snoring and slow, steady breath. He reached out to the sheet and pulled it aside to see Sid in the next bed, fast asleep.

Then he heard another sound, outside, beyond the

back door of the gym. The scrape of metal, like an old window closing.

He slipped on his shoes and grabbed his jacket off the rack, putting it on over his pajamas.

Alex tiptoed into the corridor of white sheets that ran the length of the gym, looking up and down the line. No static in his head. But now he heard a door closing somewhere. He reached back into his sheeted cubicle and grabbed his go package just in case.

He began to step quickly to the back of the gym until he reached the metal door at the rear. He opened it and peered out into the night.

Across the lawn, under the moonlight, there were no lights on in the main house of LaLaurie. Off to the right was a gate, and beyond it the woods. He let the door shut behind him and pulled the jacket closer, wishing he had put on jeans over his flannel pajama bottoms.

In the darkness a shimmer of cloth gleamed, satin, legs moving steadily and slowly, next to the gate. Not just one. As his eyes adjusted, Alex became aware that he could see three different pairs of legs crossing the small drive beyond the gate, going into the woods.

A window scraped open at the house. Alex stuck to the wall and saw a girl in pajamas, climbing through an open window, rolling and dropping silently. He recognized her—she was tall with chestnut hair and Asian features. He'd seen her at the library. She began to walk, steadily and without a glance in any direction. Alex realized with shock that she was barefoot. He could see his own breath; she must be freezing.

Not far from her window he saw several more standing open. One of them was broken, and there was a robe caught on it. *What the hell?*

He heard footsteps from around the gym, off to his right, and shrank back into the shadows. More girls, two of them, one about sixteen, the other about eighteen, both brunettes. Both barefoot, too. They walked steadily toward the gate, silently, moving through it. They came within fifty yards of him along the way and never cast him a glance.

For a moment Alex thought of running back to grab Paul and Sid, but the Asian girl and the two brunettes were still going, and he was about to lose them.

Alex ran across the lawn, looking back to see if there were any more coming. Not a soul. *Hurry.* He headed across the drive and into the woods, and was lost for a moment, perceiving no actual path. He was about to get on the ground to see if he could find footprints in the dark when he caught sight of another pair of legs in the distance, satin pajamas glimmering in the moonlight through the trees.

He made a beeline for the pajamas. He started to see more pajama'd legs, a procession up ahead. Alex headed off to the right, moving faster, until he was parallel to them. He stepped on a rotten branch. It snapped loudly, but not one of them noticed.

Now Alex saw them more clearly. There had to be a dozen or so young women, all walking neatly side by side. They seemed unconscious—he caught sight of the two brunettes he had seen earlier and they looked neither at each other nor at the girls ahead. Their eyes shimmered, unseeing, as they passed like ghosts between the trees.

Then he gasped when he saw Minhi. She was halfway up the line, and walking barefoot, wearing racing green pajamas. Her sleeve was torn where she must have had trouble getting out her window. He could see a rough scrape, visible on her exposed shoulder.

"Minhi!" he whispered. He dared to get closer to them, walking quickly, keeping trees between them. "Minhi!"

She didn't respond. He stopped for a second, hugging a tree and looking back at the procession. He stepped out, now right next to the girls as he let Minhi move on ahead. He walked for a moment alongside a pair of girls he vaguely recognized from his literature class. He waved his hand. No one glanced at him. Alex turned and stumbled up next to Minhi again. "What are you doing?" he asked.

Minhi was walking, her arms swinging slowly, a perfect automaton stride. She didn't look his way. He snapped his fingers in front of her face. "Hey!"

Nothing. *All right, that's enough.* Alex stepped in front of her this time, grabbing her left shoulder.

Minhi struck his forearm with her right. Then Alex felt the flat of her left hand smack hard against his jaw and the side of his head. No sooner had he lost his grip on her when Minhi's right arm swung back, smacking him again and sending him reeling against a tree. This little demonstration of *Hung Gar* kung fu completed, she continued on her way. He stuck to the tree and stared. Minhi hadn't looked at him once.

Alex considered retrieving something from the backpack, maybe a flash-bang, of which he had two. They did no real damage but were loud and flashy, and he could set off one and maybe break them out of their trance. But if that worked, he might not learn just what this was about.

Alex changed tactics. He started walking alongside the procession again, passing it quickly on the right. He moved steadily until he drew near the front.

They continued into the woods, barefoot, feet squishy in the soft earth, gaining scratches as they occasionally stepped on twigs. Approximately fifteen minutes, about a mile.

Then Alex saw light—several lights, in fact, torches glowing yellow through the trees. He hunkered behind a tree, staring, as the procession passed him again. They were pouring into a clearing in the woods.

Alex crept forward slowly now because they were fanning out and he couldn't see past them. He heard someone clear her throat, and he realized that all along the way he had not heard that sound. The sleeping didn't do that.

Alex reached the clearing and circled around it, trying to find the edge of the group. He heard someone yell. It was a stifled scream, like someone shouting through a gag. He started moving faster until he finally reached the edge and saw what the procession was gathered around.

There was a chair in the grass, with a man of about fifty sitting in it—no, not just sitting: tied, bound, and gagged. The man was trying to get away, but the chair was reinforced at the back and it barely rocked as he fought against the binds. He was wearing slacks and a light jacket. His eyes swiveled in terror.

Next to him was a table, and Alex saw the glint of steel—no less than ten knives laid out in a row.

Behind the chair was another table, with what looked like a pair of speakers and a small device, something that might have been an iPod. There was a figure with her back turned to them, but the hiss of static in his head and the white robes she wore identified her instantly.

Elle turned around and looked at the crowd.

"I'm going to play something for you," said Elle. "And then we're going to have a demonstration."

Chapter 18

Elle hadn't seen him. Alex thought that she would normally be able to smell him, probably from memory, but he judged that the number of mortal humans around must have been overwhelming. All that hot blood, and he was just one of many.

The man in the chair was struggling, trying to break free. Elle said, "Shh."

Alex needed to get in there and set the guy free. Right away. But what was his opening? Elle stepped back to the device that looked like an iPod and pressed its button. At once Alex heard a voice filling the clearing, liquid and golden.

"Good evening," the voice said. "I am very pleased to

see you all. You are going to do something that will set you free from all the forces that hold you down. Something you want to do—something I reveal that comes from within you."

Alex knew that voice. It was the sound of Ultravox.

But the voice was not aimed at him this time—it held no purchase on his mind as it had on the train. The voice was working on the rest of its audience, though. Alex was amazed that Ultravox could aim his message so directly; it seemed that he was specifically targeting human girls. He wondered if Ultravox could tune it by age as well, and where the hypnotic effect came in—it wasn't in the mere words, surely, because Alex was hearing the same words. He had a suspicion that Ultravox's power was more complex than that—a mixture of words and sound and possibly even some kind of psychic "hook."

And why not? Icemaker had been able to float off the ground and turn the air to ice—was it so hard to imagine vampires could learn to do all kinds of things that normal men could not?

Alex listened as the droning went on, repeating the basic idea several times, *freedom through doing what I say.* He had to admire the gall in that kind of doublethink.

"My assistant is going to give you the tools. What you want to do now is take this knife," said the voice. Alex felt his eyes grow wide as one of the girls stepped forward. Elle held out one of the silver daggers. At the edge of the knife table was a silver box, and now Elle opened that as well, revealing many, many more blades.

The girl—a senior, by the look of her, with shoulder-length strawberry hair—took the knife and stared blankly.

"The person you see before you is one of those who has kept you in thrall, one of the rule makers, the slave-holders, the barriers to your freedom."

Oh, boy. Alex looked at the man and wondered if in fact this guy was anything at all like that, a cop or an administrator. Probably not, and it didn't matter in the slightest, because this sleepwalking teenager was about to stab him.

"That's enough," Alex shouted, bursting through the trees. Elle hissed at him as he went for the knife first, smacking the redheaded girl's hand. She barely registered the knife flying from her hand, but then dropped to the grass and began to look for it again. Alex pushed her back, sending her falling.

The voice was still talking, now taking on a repeating refrain: "*Freedom through sacrifice, freedom through sacrifice, freedom through sacrifice."*

"Sorry, Al, but you're not invited," said Elle, and she grabbed him by the collar, dragging him back. Alex smashed against the table that held the iPod and it toppled over with the speakers, still playing. The voice went on as he grunted in pain, crunching his ribs against the table. He rolled forward, kicking at her.

"Freedom through sacrifice, freedom through sacrifice, freedom through sacrifice."

Alex picked up the table and swung it at Elle and she bashed it aside. Then she moved lightning fast and had his collar. She reared back her head, showing her fangs and driving toward his neck. Alex grabbed her chin, pushing, feeling the iron power of her neck muscles. He brought up his knees and caught her in the midsection, and as she fell back he reached through the seam in his backpack and drew out his stake, feeling the wooden handle and threading of silver that ran along its length.

He became aware of movement around him—the girls gathering close. The silver box clattered and they were groping for the knives that fell out on the grass.

"Freedom through sacrifice, freedom through sacrifice, freedom through sacrifice."

Alex lunged at Elle when suddenly someone had him

by the wrist and yanked him back, throwing him to the ground.

Alex's head smacked against the leg of the chair where the "sacrifice" still was trying to break free, and he tipped the chair over, allowing the man more protection, he hoped.

Then he looked back as a pair of legs came down around his and he saw glistening steel raised up high and ready to sink home.

It was Minhi.

Alex thrust his hands forward, grabbing her arm and her shoulder. "Minhi, no—"

Minhi was staring at him but not hearing his words. She was lost in *Freedom through sacrifice, freedom through sacrifice*, and because she was so athletic, she was already a little stronger than Alex. In the near distance, over the silent footsteps of the girls and the knives, over the voice of Ultravox, he heard Elle laughing.

Alex used all his strength to roll with Minhi, trying to push her away without doing any damage, but she came back at him, zombielike, raising the dagger.

"Minhi, it's me," Alex said, as Minhi slammed him back against the toppled table.

"*He's* the vessel," said Elle. "He is the one."

"Minhi—" Alex said, catching her wrist. She was

bearing down with the knife. "Wake up!" he shouted at her. There were others gathered around, because Elle had told them he was the one now, and they were waiting their turns.

Minhi was very close, and she drove her knees into his ribs, bringing the knife down slowly. "Minhi, wake up. It's me."

He remembered the snowstorm and the other night's helicopter rescue. "Take my hand," he said, using his other hand to reach for her free one. "Minhi, take my hand," he said again, and he felt the tip of the edge of the knife press down against his chest.

Suddenly he had a sense for why he had seen his sister's hand through the snow, or seen the chopper through the haze of Ultravox on the train. Because lies are fog, and truth could burn through it. Right?

He slipped his fingers through hers. "Minhi, take my hand!" he shouted, and then he saw it, a blink, and the pressing stopped. He saw her blink again. "Wake up, it's me," he whispered.

All at once Minhi gasped. "Alex?"

"Yes, can you get off me, please?"

She sprang off him like a rabbit, falling back, scrambling backward. Alex took the knife as Minhi dropped it and turned to the man in the chair. Alex had just reached the ropes binding the man when Elle hit him like a freight train, and he tumbled sideways with her.

Wasn't the first time he'd fallen with a knife, and his father's words echoed, *Keep the knife away from you always. If you begin to fall, remember where it is, and keep it pointed sideways.* In the microsecond he was falling Alex realized the tip of the knife in his hand was pointing toward his own ribs, and he twisted his hand out, landing hard on the forest floor.

The knife caught Elle in the side and she shrieked, spinning back in pain.

He returned to the task of freeing the man. He cut the binding ropes, saying, "Run, the road is that way." He waved in the general direction of the road. One of the girls was about to plunge a dagger into the man when Minhi, shrieking, grabbed her and pulled her away. The man scurried into the distance, gone, sure to have a tale to tell that no one would ever believe, ever. Alex tossed away the knife and grabbed his stake from the ground, looking around frantically for Elle. But she was gone.

Minhi kicked one of the girls away. She looked at him with tears in her eyes. "Alex, what's going on?"

The glazed-eyed girls were drawing closer. The voice of Ultravox still droned, "*Freedom through sacrifice, freedom through sacrifice, freedom through sacrifice.*"

"They're asleep, just don't hurt them," Alex said.

"They're not going to play that nice," Minhi responded as they backed up against the overturned tables.

Alex felt someone grab him by the shoulder and he spun, stabbing at his attacker—Elle—with his stake. He connected at the chest but she was able to shrink back. Alex reached into the pack and drew out a glass ball. He hurled it at her, catching her square in the forehead. The glass sphere of holy water burst and she screamed as it burned her forehead and dripped down her body. She fell back, crawling.

Elle wouldn't stay down long. She never did. But they had twenty sleepwalking assassins to deal with. Alex thought again of the flash-bang and yanked one from his pack, pulling the pin. "Minhi, cover your ears," he said. Then he shouted, "Wake up!"

He threw the flash-bang into the air as hard as he could and covered his ears just before it went off, but his ears rang anyway with the concussive force of the sound. Brilliant light shot through the clearing as the explosive noise reverberated, and he waited a second as the echo died down.

He looked back hopefully.

The glassy-eyed horde continued approaching, some

of them reaching down to grab extra knives from the silver box.

Well, that's disappointing.

On and on the voice of Ultravox played and they pressed in.

Alex looked back at the iPod in the grass and leapt for it. "That's enough," he said, and he snatched it up, ripping its cord loose from the speakers. Abruptly the voice stopped.

And so did the horde.

"Wake up!" he cried. Minhi was next to him, panting. The girls stood still, as if suspended on invisible wires.

And then Alex realized they were receding, turning, the ones in the back first, followed by the ones closer to him. Suddenly he remembered Elle and he turned with his stake at the ready.

But Elle was gone. And in a moment, so was the pajama horde, shrinking back into the distance.

Alex stood in the clearing next to Minhi. Suddenly she was hugging him. "Oh my God, I'm so sorry. Oh my God, I'm so sorry."

"It's okay," he said, hugging her back awkwardly. "We have to go."

They followed the horde as it moved in the same ant-like procession as before, through the woods and back to LaLaurie. Minhi clutched at Alex; he put his arm around her, though he was watching the girls pad their way silently, sleeping, even as they passed through the doors. One or two of them carried keys, surely on some unholy order, and Alex watched them unconsciously unlock the doors and enter. On up to their rooms, where, one and all, they returned to sleep.

Chapter 19

Alex slapped the purloined Scholomance device down on the conference table, right in the center of the *u* in *Talia Sunt.* He had come to HQ immediately after dropping off Minhi, calling Sangster along the way.

"What have you got there?" Armstrong said, picking it up.

The door opened and Sangster came in, wearing a sport coat and chinos and looking like he was called into meetings in the middle of the night all the time. He tossed his jacket over a chair and sat next to Alex, gazing at the small white device in Armstrong's hands from across the table.

"It's an iPod," Alex said. "Basically, I think."

Armstrong turned it over and pitched it to Sangster. It was about the size of a deck of cards, with no video screen but ports for speakers and USB. Unlike the Apple device it resembled, it had only one button.

"Elle left it behind when I disrupted her sacrifice, or whatever it was. Her directed killing."

"That was unwise of her." Sangster looked at Armstrong. "Let's have Monty look at this."

They headed out the door and down the carpeted halls until they came to an area Alex had never seen, a large bay of computers and screens and what looked like a studio mixing board.

A man with scant amounts of yellow hair and one arm looked up at them as they entered his area. He was wearing earphones and watching a screen where Alex could see various lines representing sound. The lines were pulsing, and Alex realized he was listening to music.

"Monty!" Armstrong called, and the balding man nodded distantly.

"What is it, I'm listening to—"

Armstrong tugged the earphone jack out of the mixing board and the room filled with techno. "I have actual work for you."

The guy looked at Sangster, Armstrong, and Alex,

and rolled his eyes. "This *is* work. Look at this." He pointed at the screen, indicating a low, fluid line that ran below the others. "See that little line down there? It's a conversation. I'm listening to some recordings we got last week in Geneva. Got some stuff on your Ultravox. Not much, though. Vampires, man, they go into town and talk. Don't believe the hype; they do drink wine." He slid a lever and the volume receded. He turned to Alex. "Hey, you're the Van Helsing kid."

Alex nodded. Sangster said, "This is Monty Crief, he's a communications intelligence specialist with—another agency, but we've got him for Ultravox."

So that was what they were calling the operation, Ultravox, a whole rolling chain of events captured under one name. "What is that?" Monty said, suddenly interested. Sangster tossed the device again and Monty snatched it out of the air with his one arm. *"Cool."*

Alex said, "About an hour ago a vampire from the Scholomance played whatever is on that thing for a bunch of girls in the woods. It told them to kill a man, and they almost did it."

Monty was plugging in the device. He tapped the button and the voice of Ultravox began to play. *"Freedom through sacrifice, freedom through sacrifice."*

"Gotta admit, that is one mellifluous voice," Monty

said. He started bringing up other windows.

Armstrong picked up a file off the desk area of Monty's station and flipped it open, showing Alex a pencil sketch based on the person he had seen on the train. "This is the person you saw. This is Ultravox."

"Have you matched him with anyone?" Alex asked.

"Not yet. So far this is just a guy in a peasant shirt."

Sangster looked at the picture. "If I didn't know better I'd think we were fighting Ernest Hemingway."

Alex thought of the Icemaker adventure. "Do you think we might be?"

Sangster said, "It's tempting, but no, Hemingway was not a vampire. Did some work for us, once, but that's a whole other thing."

"I'm running this through the database," said Monty. "Should just be a moment."

Alex was surprised. "You have a database of all the vampires' voices?"

"No," Monty said, "but there are a lot of elements out there that work their mojo through sound. There's a Malaysian vampire that sings, a whole clan of Benedictine monk/sorcerers in Germany that use chants, and on and on. As in life, there are people who deal in sound."

Alex turned back to Sangster and Armstrong. "Here's what I don't get. The voice told them to kill the guy, okay? And Elle brought a box of knives and laid them out for them. But *why were the girls even there*?"

Armstrong folded her arms. Her freckles showed in the dim light. "Could it have been back-masked or something, into a public announcement?"

"They don't do PAs that way at LaLaurie," Sangster said, shaking his head. "But I see where you're going."

"I don't," said Alex. "Clue me in."

"There could have been a posthypnotic suggestion sent to these girls," Sangster explained. "A message telling them to get up in the middle of the night and meet in the woods."

Alex was looking at the file in the folder. The voice of Ultravox still haunted him, and in his mind he could hear it turned on him as opposed to the message on the iPod, which was meant for the pajama horde. *It will never get better than this,* Ultravox had said.

"Only girls were there," Alex said, trying to focus on the task at hand, despite his distaste for the sound of the vampire's voice. "There are boys at LaLaurie now, but only girls went into the woods. Why would it be just girls?"

Sangster shrugged. "I don't think we have an answer for that yet."

"Would this message have to be explicit?" Alex

continued his questions. "I mean, as explicit as 'get up at one and go a mile into the woods?'"

"Maybe. Could be a virus," said Monty, who had put on a pair of headphones but could still hear them. He was sorting through several long lists of files, each bearing incomprehensible names.

Sangster had never heard of this. "A virus?"

Monty looked back, tapping a button to pause whatever he was listening to. He rubbed his forehead, clearly trying to dumb down his explanation as much as he could. "Like a computer virus. A whole set of instructions enclosed in a string of words, a magic spell, if you will. It could be in any language; if someone good—and we gotta assume Ultravox is good—he could create a posthypnotic virus that would include the instructions. All that would be left would be to inject it into the targets."

"It could be a teacher," Alex said. "A plant at LaLaurie. Or Glenarvon."

Monty held up a finger, shushing them, and unplugged his headphones.

They heard a voice on an old, crackling recording. "You are going to do something now, not for me, but because you want to."

"That's him," Alex said.

Monty played the two recordings simultaneously, and

the two droning recordings swirled over each other on the screen. "This recording was made in 1937 in Washington, D.C. It is the only known recording of Jonathan Frene."

"Frene," Sangster whispered, staring at the name that Monty brought up on the screen. A dossier followed, but there was no picture. Alex saw time lines running back hundreds of years. "Frene was a voice man?"

"You've heard of him?" Alex asked.

Sangster held up two fingers. "Two ways. One, Jonathan Frene is a name that pops up in vampire events a lot in the past couple hundred years. Assassinations, mainly. And second, he was seeded into a story by Algernon Blackwood, a writer and one of our agents in the first half of the twentieth century. He suggested a psychic vampire; that's someone who can suck out your will. Blackwood may have mislabeled him."

Armstrong was looking over the dossier on the screen. "Sometimes Frene went by Cracknell."

"That's familiar," Alex said, puzzled, then whispered rapidly, "Cracknell, Cracknell." Something recent. White embossed words on leather.

It's a theory book, he heard Sid say.

Alex racked his brain. "Did Frene write any books himself?"

"Not that I'm familiar with," said Sangster.

Armstrong peered at the screen. "There's a long letter he wrote to one of the clans in 1901 listed here. Says it got passed around a lot. It was called The Skein."

"The Skein," Alex repeated. "Oh my God."

"What?"

"Sid found a book at the bookstore in Secheron on writing when we were looking for materials for the Pumpkin Show. It was a writing book, you know, for making stories. It was called *The Skein*, with some kind of subtitle."

Sangster looked visibly saddened. "*The Skein* was never really published. Sid has been using this book?"

"Yes, and when he reads his stories the audience practically swoons. He's competing regularly now. I think he has a shot to win."

Armstrong snorted. "There's your virus," she said. "So what do you know about this Sid?"

"This Sid?" Alex repeated indignantly.

"Is he a vampire fan, maybe could be turned?"

"No, no," Alex said. "No, he—he's a fan, but he thinks it's all fiction. Or he did. But no, it can't be that."

"I agree," Sangster said. "I've known him for two years. He's a solid young man."

Monty was nodding excitedly. "With a book—with

a book, it's easier. Here's how this would work, in a nutshell: Your friend gets the book. He reads from the book. The spell gets into his head. He writes things down that are influenced by the book—maybe subtly, maybe just a few words, maybe just syllables. He reads them aloud and they get heard by the girls who were the targets. And, mind you, they would be *targets*. It would be aimed at them. The girls then do whatever simple task the virus told them to do—in this case, to go wait for further instructions."

Monty opened his hands and smiled, pleased by the cleverness of this thing that Alex didn't find all that pleasing. "With a book, it's easier," he said again.

There was a buzz in Sangster's pocket and he fished his cell phone out, glancing down. "The victim just came in."

"Came in?" Alex asked.

"Yeah," Sangster said. "I'll deal with that."

"So you tell us," Armstrong continued. "How is it that of all the gin joints in the world, Sid walks into Ultravox's?" Alex looked puzzled, and she clarified. "Why did your friend pick *that* book?"

Alex replayed the moment in his head. They had been at the bookstore, and Sid and Alex had joined the others upstairs. Everyone was looking at *Master Plots* and Sid wanted something else. And suddenly, there had been a book thrust into his hands.

"He didn't," Alex realized. He threw his backpack over his shoulder. "Someone picked it for him. And you know what else? *Vienna* didn't go in the woods, either."

Chapter 20

Vienna's scarf—that had to be the key. Chances are she was marked, already a—a thrall, was what Sid had called it, a live servant of the Scholomance who went about her day surreptitiously taking orders, waiting for the moment she would become a vampire. Sid had laid it out for him, without even knowing he was being used. She'd probably been bitten, poisoned. And set loose among them. And he'd sent Minhi up to sleep in a room with her!

In the morning Alex hurried to breakfast and the coming battle, prepared for anything. He even brought his go package just in case, tucked inside his school backpack.

When he entered the dining hall, his eyes swept the room, looking for the faces of the girls he had seen the night before. Here and there he recognized them, chatting and talking as though everything was normal. None returned his gaze with anything approaching recognition or guilt.

He spotted the table along the wall where Minhi was sitting with Sid, Paul, and Vienna. As Alex approached, two girls came up to Sid.

"Oh, hey," Sid said, shrinking a little. The two girls giggled and one of them asked him to sign a program from the last Pumpkin Show. He smiled, his ginger hair flopping about, and obliged, shrugging and laughing as if embarrassed. When they scampered away Minhi reached over and punched him in the shoulder, giggling.

"Minhi," Alex said, taking a chair at the corner. They all greeted him, but Alex didn't hear, distracted. He was searching Minhi's eyes for a signal, some remembrance of the nightmare they had shared.

"You look awful," Paul said. "You should eat something before you blow away."

"I didn't get much sleep," Alex said.

"You're telling me," Paul responded. For a moment Alex wondered if he was aware, if somehow Minhi had already told him. Paul continued, "Those sheets are driving me insane. I feel like we're in some kind of hospital."

Alex shrugged, looked back at Minhi. "How about you?"

"Me?" Minhi stopped, mid-chew. She gestured with her toast. "I swear you can hear the snoring coming all the way from Boys Town, but that might just be Vienna."

Alex blinked. Vienna frowned with worry. "Alex, what's wrong?"

"It's, uh . . ."—he looked at Minhi again—"do you have a sec? I wanted to ask you about something." He felt himself making a face that was obvious and huge, and she put down her toast.

"I'm gonna get some more juice," she said slowly.

Paul watched them go with interest but then went back to talking to Sid.

Alex walked with her. "So?" he said. They reached the serving table where an orange juice dispenser sat next to a neat stack of glasses.

"So?" she repeated.

"So, what are we gonna say? How are we gonna do this?"

Minhi thrust her glass under the dispenser, her narrow face showing confusion and a hint of irritation. "What are you talking about?"

"Did you already tell Paul? Listen, Vienna might be compromised. I mean, you know, she might be in on it."

"You're acting really weird, Alex," she said, and she poured him some orange juice.

Alex took the glass, staring at her. It was impossible to imagine that she didn't remember a thing. "You walked back with me. You were *awake*."

"What?" Minhi looked back at their table and for a moment he felt sure she was going to drop the facade; surely this was a ruse because she had already figured out that certain people couldn't be trusted. "I don't know what you're trying to say or do, but I don't like it."

Alex's heart sank with realization. He had to try once more. "You don't remember any of it?"

"I don't know what you're talking about," Minhi said, and her eyes looked a little sad. "And it's really kind of getting upsetting."

"Okay," he said. "It's just . . ." What was there to say? She had erased the whole thing. The same vocal virus that had woken up the girls had also erased the entire event once they went back to sleep. He was certain of it; she wasn't faking.

They got back to the table and Alex sat down with his orange juice.

"Look at this," Paul said, gesturing at him. "A

breakfast consisting entirely of liquid. I think maybe *you're* a vampire."

Alex dutifully smiled, but he caught Vienna's eye. She looked concerned, as though she had been watching them the whole time. "I was just asking Minhi if maybe we can do something to celebrate Sid's newfound celebrity," Alex said as another girl tapped Sid on the shoulder and gave him the thumbs-up.

"There's another reading this weekend," Paul said brightly. "You got a new one, then?"

"There's something new," Sid said. "This one is about music."

"Oooh, sounds cool," Paul said, clearly proud of his friend's accomplishments. "If it's already written, maybe we can all hang out tonight. The ball's not till tomorrow."

"Perfect," said Alex. Perfect, except that Sid was passing along a spell. He was Typhoid Sid.

"These stories you do are *like* music," Vienna said, smiling. "But as a Spaniard I'm waiting for one about the tango."

Everyone in the room started to jostle and rise, and Minhi looked at her watch. It was time for class. Alex realized on top of everything else, he was hungry after all. But it had to wait.

They began carrying their trays to the front of the dining hall, and Alex came up next to Vienna. "Vienna."

"Alex," she replied, almost officiously, responding to the tone he'd taken.

"Can we talk?" he said.

Vienna stopped and put down her tray, turning to him brightly. "Absolutely."

Alex nodded good-bye to the others, and he and Vienna walked out of the dining hall in silence. He saw Paul throw him the thumbs-up and Alex rolled his eyes. They got out into the hall and he stopped by a tall window near a door. "I need you to do something."

"I have already given up a sleeve," Vienna said, laughing.

"I need you to take off your scarf."

Vienna maintained her cheerful grin. "Never, it's my air of mystery."

"Vienna," Alex said seriously. "Please." He knew exactly what he was going to see. He wasn't sure if the marks—fang marks, delivering the poison—would be new or old, but he knew they would be there.

The smile drained from her face. "Alex, please, I can't. Don't ask me."

"Please don't say that," Alex said. Opening the door, he led her outside where he was able to raise his voice.

"Look, I don't know what's going on, but I think you're not a . . . a bad person, but I need you to do this."

She started walking away. "Leave me alone."

"Vienna, if you're in some kind of trouble, I can help. I can help you."

"Leave me alone!"

"Take off your scarf!"

"You don't know what you're asking."

Vienna was running now, and Alex chased after her. She ran across the lawn and picked up speed, and he followed. She ran until she had stopped in the woods, her back turned to him. He saw her head wobbling, as if she was crying.

Alex stopped behind her, panting for breath. "I just need to know if you're one of them."

"I can't. It's not time, maybe someday it will be time, but it's not time."

He came around in front of her. "Just this once."

"Alex!" She seemed so vulnerable, and he kept his hands down.

He wasn't about to take the scarf from her by force. "Look, I can't make you," Alex said. "I won't make you. But I need you to show me. I need you to take off the scarf."

"It's not time."

"I saved your life!" he said. "I thought Elle was going to kill you."

"And what?" she said. "I owe you?"

This caught him like a slap in the face and he felt instantly ashamed. "They're good people," Alex said, looking down. "Sid and Paul and Minhi. I'm worried and I think this is the answer. Please."

Vienna put her hands to her eyes. After a long moment, she sighed and reached down. In one deft flick she pulled the scarf loose. It flowed like a streamer to the earth, green and shimmering.

And then her head fell off.

Chapter 21

His first reaction was to scream, and that was something Alex Van Helsing didn't actually do very much. He had been grabbed at in the dark by zombies and nearly eaten by giant dogs from hell, but screaming was not a part of the sequence. It was always, *What's next, what do you have?* But when Vienna's head popped off her body like the heaviest part of a china doll whose neck had gotten frayed, he actually did yelp and stagger back.

And then it kicked in, the same leveling in his blood, the same words his father had taught him when he found himself on a cliff and the branch he'd grabbed was starting to pull loose, when the rock he was on started to crumble, when he was faced with a test question he never prepared for. *Breathe. That sudden rush of blood is your trigger to listen and look and breathe. The world will want you to be pulled along. You must breathe, and ask the questions.*

What is happening?

The girl lay on the forest floor as though she had been knocked out, one arm underneath her and the other stretched out. As though she had simply dropped asleep.

Vienna's head, as cleanly excised as a pat of butter, had rolled to a stop against a tree. There was zero gore. Instead, an inch below Vienna's jaw, where the neck both began and ended, there shimmered a green field, almost like a violin bow resin.

On the body, the solid edge of Vienna's neck was the same, neatly ending in another shimmering green field. Alex gingerly reached out and took Vienna's wrist, feeling for a pulse.

Jiminy Cricket. The girl's heart was beating. *Okay. What is happening?*

What is happening is that this is magic.

Magic. Just one more thing that wasn't supposed to be, except now he knew that vampires used it all the time. They used it to hide the vast Scholomance under the lake, and used it to concoct worms of blood. His *mother* used magic, and there were others like her, apparently.

And Vienna, it appeared, used it to keep her head from rolling away from her body.

Alex reached over and delicately closed Vienna's staring eyes. That was tough. The urge to lose it began again for a second. *Think. You didn't do this.*

But you did! You made her—

You made her take off the scarf.

A breeze blew through the woods, lifting leaves, and Alex's eyes darted to Vienna's scarf, which picked up and began to blow.

She pulled off the scarf. She needs it.

And it was blowing away. Alex went after the scarf as it began to lift into the air. It blew a few more feet and hung on a tree, threatening to disappear into the woods.

He stepped over to the tree and took the scarf. Did it somehow, what, hold her head on? It wasn't like tape or anything; it felt like a scarf, like something his twin sister would have picked up in Milan. Alex touched the scarf and it began to leap again, more deliberately this time, like a small animal. He barely closed his fingers around it when it broke free, shooting off onto the grass. The shimmering green scarf began to slide, snakelike, along the ground.

Alex had to jump this time to grab it before it disappeared under the leaves. It was headed deeper into the woods. He had the distinct impression it was heading for the lake.

Alex reemerged in the clearing with the scarf whipping about in his hands. It was strong, but still just cloth; it had no teeth to dig into his skin. It wanted to get away.

The scarf stopped struggling for a moment and it merely twisted, slowly, pulsing in his hands.

Who in the world was Vienna Cazorla? She had a beating heart, but was it even real? Was she some creature placed here by the vampires? Or maybe that thing Sid had mentioned—was she a *thrall*?

Don't get distracted. You won't know that unless you can help, and if her heart is beating you can help.

Alex felt something at his throat. He looked down to see that the scarf had almost inched its way out of his fingers and was tickling at his throat, trying to slide around it.

He clenched his fingers around the scarf and held it at a distance. It twitched in the air. He had a feeling that if he let it get to him, he'd be the one rocking a jaunty green scarf from then on out. Which might look swell, but there'd still be a headless girl with a beating heart in the woods, so—

Time to give it back?

Absolutely.

Alex approached Vienna's body while he held the scarf away from him with one hand.

He was breaking all kinds of rules. Body in the woods, you call EMS, you don't go rearranging it. Except every rule was finished now. He could have moved the head more easily, but he just couldn't will himself to pick Vienna's head up by her hair.

And anyway, he had a feeling it wasn't a "body." It was a girl with some explaining to do.

Now or never. Either this would work or he was absolutely screwed.

She was fairly light, especially missing about nine pounds. He knelt down into the grass in his dress pants—*Crap, I'm missing class*—reaching his arm under her shoulders and across her chest, and gingerly moved her lower six-sevenths, bringing it to rest just next to the head.

The scarf began to twitch again when he held it near her, reaching out. He released the scarf and stepped away. It wrapped instantly around Vienna's neck and head. Silence.

Double crap.

Then, there was a faint static pop and Vienna blinked twice. She awoke as if she had dozed off and stared at Alex, before instantly scrambling back against the tree.

"What is going on?" Vienna demanded.

Alex dropped to his knees. *I cannot believe that worked.* "Oh, thank God. Oh my *God.*"

Vienna's eyes widened with horror as she grasped for her throat.

"Say something," he said. "Are you . . . I mean, are you okay?"

"What did you *do*?" Vienna demanded. She was reaching around her neck, feeling at it when Alex saw her remember. When she looked back up Alex was expecting her to blaze with fury, but what he saw was tempered with misery.

"I'm sorry," Alex said. He helped her up, and Vienna brushed at her clothing. "I didn't know. I had no idea."

"Really?" Vienna asked, the *r* rolling with anger. She inspected the huge smudges on her elbows and heels. "All of that 'Take off your scarf' and you didn't know?"

"I thought you were a vampire."

"You can *sense* vampires," Vienna said.

"Or a *thrall* or something. Okay, I'm sorry," Alex said, but he was already past his relief. "Don't make this about me, Vienna. Right now there's something terrible going on, and it all started with a book that *you* put in Sid's hands."

Vienna stopped. "This shouldn't have happened."

Alex had to nod. "Yeah, I know. Vienna? Seriously. You have to tell me what's going on."

She said in frustration, "I didn't want anyone to get hurt."

"So tell me you're not working for the Scholomance."

"I'm not working *for* them," Vienna said at last. "But I guess you could say that I am in their thrall."

And then she told her story.

Chapter 22

Vienna Cazorla was rowing at dusk in the pond at Retiro Park when she first saw the vampire. It was summer in Madrid, and the evening air was cool, the water dark and motionless as her rowboat slowly edged across it. It was strange to be rowing alone, but then she felt strange.

Rowing was the only thing she had thought to do, the only thing that made sense. Vienna had rushed out of the hospital, feeling sick herself. She had been to see her brother, and now she wanted to do something that he should be doing with her. She was aching and wanted to act out the ache with her arms, using oars he should be using.

Carlos was dying. He was a National Guardsman and

that had always been such a glorious thing; she had loved to see him in his dashing uniform, loved the chocolates he brought back from wherever he went. But he had been caught in a blast when terrorists in the north blew up a car next to a small bodega where he had been getting a take-out order of paella. Carlos had not even been on duty. It was chance alone that had struck him with chunks of concrete and fire and bashed in his skull. He lingered in the hospital in Madrid, maybe aware of his parents, maybe aware of Vienna. Maybe.

She had run from the hospital and rented a boat and furiously swept herself to the center, in the shadow of the Prado Museum, surrounded by trees and dying light.

The sound of tourists and picnicking families, the chirping of birds, the quiet stroke of the oars, all of it mocked her, normal and everyday, obscenely oblivious to her pain. Nothing was normal anymore.

She barely noticed the girl on the shore; with her eyes she swept over the spiky blond hair and the white coat and didn't look again. Vienna may have been aware the girl was watching her, but maybe that was something she realized only later. Vienna swore angrily as she rowed. There was no one to talk to. Her parents were in their own world. Her friends at school—there really wasn't such a thing at the moment, because school was over, and when she returned she'd be at a new place, at LaLaurie School for Girls, and the cast would change.

She missed Steven, the American she had known at Vogler Academy, her primary school in Switzerland. Steven was quiet, and he had always listened, but recently she had sent letters and he hadn't failed to answer so much as failed to answer in any meaningful way. He was changing, and what had been silence in person had become a distant dryness on paper. No. There was no one left but her brother, and he was dying.

Vienna moored the boat as it grew dark and walked past the Prado, down thin Madrid streets, past restaurant owners beckoning tourists to dinner, the expensive *menús del día* around the park, and farther back, where the locals gathered and drank and ate, better menus and better prices.

She found herself in a small, cramped museum that had been a favorite of Carlos's, one they had visited just before he headed north. She found herself wandering through the etchings of Goya, *Los Caprichos*, the capricious, the random, and evil. Garish faces and unhappy people, the accidents of life.

And then she found herself in front of *The Resurrection of Lazarus*. It was a painting in the style of El Greco, elongated figures and vibrant, garish color. Vienna had seen countless paintings on the subject, but it had been Carlos who had drawn her to this one: Jesus before the tomb, Lazarus the dead, standing barely inside behind the rolled-away stone. Lazarus was wrapped head to foot in white shrouds, and as he looked out, walking toward the beckoning Christ, his face was ghoulish and green, and full of horror. It was a painting that spoke of shock and blasphemy. Lazarus was risen, barely able to comprehend: *Who has done this thing? You who are so powerful, why have you done this? Did the people who love me so know what they have done? What a curse it is to return to this world?*

A minor *Lazarus*, but a shocking one.

"That is one unhappy dead man," the person behind her said, in perfect Spanish, and that was when she met Elle.

Elle, whose eyes shone brilliantly and huge in a face of chalky white skin. Vienna found herself listening to her. Elle said, "I want to talk to you about your brother."

It only took an hour. Elle led her to a quiet café where she told her what she had in mind. She did not hypnotize and yet she was hypnotic.

"We can save him," Elle said, "but of course it's forbidden, and all forbidden things have a price. There is a curse you must take on yourself in exchange for his."

Anything. She would do anything.

"And one day, some day, we will ask a favor of you," Elle said.

An inkling of the limits of her blasphemy flashed across Vienna's mind. "You're going to ask me to kill someone," she said.

"Doesn't have to be that," Elle said in her curious casual way. "No, it will be a simple favor."

"When can you help Carlos?" Vienna said.

"We can do it tonight," Elle said.

"He won't die?"

"He won't," Elle said, "not for a long time."

"When will your request come?"

Elle reached under the table and took out a silver box, which she slid across the table, next to Vienna's water glass. At her request, Vienna opened the box and saw inside, laid in black velvet, a shimmering green scarf. "The first one comes as soon as you say you're in," Elle said. "And that's as simple as putting this little present on. The next request—we'll let you know."

Carlos recovered. He recovered fast, with a voracious appetite. He healed like no one the doctors had ever seen before. It was with joy that she bade him good-bye in the fall, he teasing her about her newfound accessory, which she never took off, ever.

And on the evening Vienna heard that the school across the lake had suffered a severe fire, she received her next instructions.

Elle provided Vienna with a target, always intended to be someone who could write and who could get in front of the students of LaLaurie. Elle had a handful of candidates—had even made sure Vienna roomed with one—but none of them was quite the perfect vessel for the Ultravox virus. Within hours of the fire, when it became clear that boys would be moving to LaLaurie, a stack of new dossiers landed in Elle's lap. And when she came across Sid's dossier Elle rejected all of the previous candidates. Sid studied vampires, had even read some vampire writing, and his head would already be seeded with keywords and phrases. He would be susceptible, even if only slightly more so, to the kind of subconscious suggestion that Ultravox planned to utilize. And he spent a great deal of time writing. Sid would be perfect. All that was left was for Vienna to watch for an opportunity.

Chapter 23

Vienna and Alex found Sid, Paul, and Minhi coming out of class and hurried them in the opposite direction of the moving crowds.

Sid was already walking with them but looked back. "Don't we have to get to class?"

"Oh, we're being all kinds of truant today," Alex said. They snuck out the side exit and headed across the lawn to New Aubrey House, where no one would be working until the afternoon.

As Alex started a fire in the fireplace of the small, dusty study, Minhi beheld the scuffs and smudges all over Vienna with shock. "What happened to you?"

"I lost my head," said Vienna.

Alex stoked the fire and looked back at Sid and his backpack. "Do you have the book?"

Sid somehow knew the one he was talking about and fished it out. It was dog-eared and full of papers he had stuck in it. Sid laid it on the table. "Yep."

Alex explained bluntly. "The book is a plant," he said. "It's magic, vampire magic. The kind that powerful vampires have access to, just as powerful as the spells that keep the Scholomance entrance hidden. But *this* magic was aimed at us—at students. Sid, I'm really sorry, but the book has a sort of virus in it, and it's been passing through you to students at LaLaurie."

"It's my fault," Vienna said. "I gave you the book."

"Randomly?" Sid asked evenly. He had a pale, sick look about him.

"No," she said. "The vampire girl—Elle—made me do it. She saved my brother's life and demanded that I do her a favor in return. That favor was to make sure that someone used the book in the Pumpkin Show." She looked miserable. "I'm so sorry; I had no idea what she had planned."

Minhi visibly shrank from her friend, but Alex held up his hands, as if somehow he could take fear away by waving his fingers. "It's not Vienna's fault," Alex said. "We all know what the Scholomance is capable of. You all know—actually, I guess you don't know all of it." He looked at Minhi. "When you woke up this morning, was there anything strange?"

Minhi looked sheepish. "I'm sorry?"

"There was, wasn't there?"

"Dirt. There was dirt. I couldn't explain it, but there didn't seem to be any reason to bring up to you that my feet were dirty."

Alex folded over in his head how deep he felt like going into the narrative of the last twenty-four hours and finally said, "The stories Sid has been writing using the outlines in the book have put a posthypnotic suggestion in some of our heads. *Which* some would be: girls. It seems to have only affected girls, and I'm not sure why. Last night, Minhi, you and a lot of other girls walked into the woods. And came back and didn't remember a thing."

"I went into the woods?" Minhi asked. She pulled her jacket closer. "What did—what did I do there?"

"Nothing permanent," Alex said.

"Were you there?" Paul asked. There was an edge of betrayal in his voice.

"Yes," Alex answered. "And so was Elle. Elle was trying to give them . . . more instructions. I disrupted her and everyone went home," he summed up.

"Oh my God," Minhi said. "What are we going to do?"

"The book is by Ultravox, isn't it? The guy on the train, who nearly talked you into throwing yourself off?" Sid said, rising to pick up the leather volume. "It says David Cracknell is the author."

"A pseudonym." Alex nodded. "His real name is Jonathan Frene."

Sid snorted in frustration. "Gyahhh."

"What?" Alex asked.

"*Again* with the superhero names throwing us off. Ultravox he's gotta go by. And Cracknell. But Jonathan Frene? As in Algernon Blackwood's *The Transfer*?"

Paul raised a hand. "Mind cluing us lesser intellects in, mate?"

"It's a classic—very old—vampire story," said Sid, pacing before the fire with the book. "*The Transfer* tells the story of Jonathan Frene, a man who sucks the energy out of everyone he comes close to. He's a psychic vampire. He nearly kills the narrator's family."

Alex's interest was piqued. "How do they defeat him?"

"They don't." Sid looked into the fire. "He's a blank. All he is is what he takes. All he feels is what he makes others feel. In the end, he's sucked away himself by a more powerful psychic force."

"What kind of psychic force?"

Sid thought for a moment, clearly trying to explain it. "A dead spot," he said. "I mean, it's an allegory. They drag him to a place that's desolate and can't grow anything and all the energy flows out of him."

"Anyone know where I can get one of these allegories?" Alex clasped his hands. "And can you put it on a crossbow?"

Sid clenched his fists. "I can't believe it!"

"Hey, hey," Paul said.

"I thought I was . . ." He shook his head, trailing off. His eyes were big and sad. "I mean, I thought I was good."

"You are good," Minhi said. "It's an outline book. It can't *give* you mad writing skills."

"I agree," Alex said. "Sid, I talked to people who know about this. The book passed a virus of sorts through you. But Minhi's right; the talent behind the stories; that would be your own. It's just a crutch," Alex said.

Sid looked at the book for a moment, flopping it over on the love seat. "Then I don't need it," he said. He turned and threw it into the fire.

They all watched the book for a few minutes as the flames caught the edges. It writhed and curled as if alive, but unlike Vienna's scarf, this was just an effect of old paper and leather and fire.

"Then that's that," Alex said. "Frene is not getting in this way again."

"Not through us, he's not," Paul said.

"What now?" Minhi asked, looking at Alex. She was sitting on the edge of the couch as if ready to spring, but there was nowhere to spring to.

Alex sat back, feeling totally exhausted. He'd gotten almost no sleep the night before. "The Polidorium wants to know why Ultravox hypnotized a bunch of girls. They're working on it."

Sid picked up his backpack, shaking his head. "I'm going to have to write an all-new story for the last round. I don't even know when there'll be a chance to do it. Certainly not until after the ball."

"The ball!" Alex slapped his forehead. "My God, is it me or do we keep an insane calendar?"

"All I know is if we don't eat lunch I'm going to strangle someone," Paul said.

"Good, because I'm *starving*," Alex said.

As they walked back to the cafeteria, Alex felt his cell phone buzz in his pocket and retrieved it, reading a text message. He turned to Vienna and said, "Listen—do you like motorcycles?"

Chapter 24

After lunch and class, Alex and Vienna walked to the woods, Alex carrying a duffel bag. Once out of sight of the school Alex pulled two motorcycle helmets from the bag and led her to the Ninja. Vienna eyed the machine warily. It had room enough for an extra person, at least a smallish extra person.

"Just keep your feet back and don't touch the exhaust," Alex said, handing the extra helmet to her. He had kept the extra helmet (another loan, gift, whatever, from the Polidorium) in his new footlocker and frankly expected it to remain unused. As Vienna put it on, the black plastic covered everything but the green scarf. He had the impression of headless Vienna again, a ghoulish thought that was so bizarre it almost made him laugh out loud.

He kept the Ninja to a leisurely speed on the road to Secheron Village, watching the trees and light traffic whiz past. Vienna kept her arms wrapped around his waist.

"Where are we going?" Vienna shouted in Alex's ear. He could barely hear her over the sound of the engine.

"To see a friend," Alex shouted back.

"Why do you keep your motorcycle hidden in the woods?" Vienna asked, and even over the roar of the engine he could hear the charming *j* in *jor motorcycle.*

"I haven't figured out yet how to explain it," Alex answered. "It's kind of for work."

"Does everyone ride a motorcycle at your work?" She laughed, giddy.

"Even the bad guys. Elle has a Ducati; it's pretty sweet. Well, she did. It blew up. Don't think about that."

They came up behind an old, tiny Peugeot and buzzed around it, picking up speed, and after that there was not a soul until they hit the village. No killer Mercedes or worm bombs or anything.

They swept into Village Square at around four thirty and cruised uptown, along the street where he had chased Elle, to the marina. Sangster was waiting at the café on the marina, sitting at a gleaming steel table with someone Alex did not recognize right away.

As Alex parked he studied the man with Sangster—about fifty, silver hair and a mustache, blue suit and a trench coat, gray eyes. Then it hit him.

Sangster laid down his menu, gesturing at two empty chairs. "Alex, Vienna," he said, as he and the other man both rose. "Please sit."

"Mr. Sangster." Vienna shook his hand.

Sangster introduced them. "This is Vienna Cazorla and Alex Van Helsing. You've heard of both of them."

"Of course," the man said, taking a pair of small wire glasses out of his pocket and putting them on before shaking their hands.

"And this is Professor Nathan Montrose of Oxford University." Sangster sat back down.

Alex shook the professor's hand and kept his eyes on him as he backed into his chair. They sat in silence for a moment. Alex finally said, "Uh, well, I'm glad you're alive."

Montrose's mouth moved into a smile and then he laughed heartily, clapping his hands as he repeated it to Sangster. "He's glad I'm alive. Very good. Very good. Me too."

Vienna cleared her throat, which Alex took to mean, *Clue me in, anyone?*

"This is the guy from the woods," Alex said.

"Oh, my," Vienna gasped. She clapped her fingers together and brought them to her lips. "Professor, I didn't know what was going to happen. I'm so sorry."

Sangster patted her forearm. "It's all right. The professor reported in this morning and told us what had happened. That's when we put it together."

"Put what together?" Alex asked. He still couldn't figure out why Sangster would want them to meet what he had thought had been a random victim. But now it appeared that the Polidorium knew him.

The professor said, "Vienna, is it?" She nodded and he continued, "You were just a pawn for the Scholomance."

Sangster said, "Professor Montrose is an expert on the Scholomance and has been conducting research for us in England. He's been the target of several assassination attempts because he's building a—let's just say a new tool that will prove very useful." Alex guessed Sangster was referring to Chatterbox.

"All in half a lifetime's work." The professor smiled.

"Ultravox was here to assassinate you so that the expert behind the database would be out of commission," Alex said. "Assassinate you using *teenagers*."

"Right," said Sangster.

Alex thought about the events in the woods. "But

why?" he asked. "I mean, why couldn't Elle have just done it?"

"Right now we're going on the because-it's-dramatic theory," Sangster said. "I know it's unsatisfactory."

"Let me see if I understand this theory," Alex said. "The Scholomance knows that Professor Montrose is coming to Geneva. They want to assassinate him. So they bring in Ultravox to perform the assassination, and Ultravox devises a plan to recruit teenagers at the local girls' school. He creates a vocal virus, a hypnotic spell, for them all to hear, and ensures that the book with the virus in it is put into the hands of someone who will be speaking to them all."

Montrose flopped over a pair of gloves on the table. "And then once the virus is in their heads, Ultravox gives them the instructions. His voice is essentially unignorable. No one can overcome it, Alex. His voice threads the brain with his will, until you can't hear anything else."

"But there are boys at LaLaurie now. Boys are bigger. If Ultravox wanted to use students, boys might have given them a physical edge," Alex said.

"You're forgetting that you guys weren't supposed to be at LaLaurie," Sangster said. "The plan to pass the book to someone presenting to students was keyed on

LaLaurie. It was aimed at girls."

"What happened to the book you were given?" Professor Montrose interjected, leaning forward.

"Uh . . ." Alex realized that maybe destroying it hadn't been the best course. It could have proved useful.

"We burned it," Vienna said. Her brow was knitted with fury at having been manipulated by these people, and her tone said she didn't regret destroying the book at all.

Montrose sighed, disappointed. "Ah, well. Undoubtedly we'll find another copy."

"What's next for Ultravox?" Alex said.

Sangster shook his head. "All the chatter on him is quiet now. That either means he's looking for a new way to get at Nathan or the Scholomance has no more use for him now that he's failed this attempt."

Montrose nodded in agreement. "I wouldn't be surprised if we pick up that Ultravox will be . . . *punished* for that failure."

Alex felt oddly unconvinced, but he didn't have a better theory to suggest. A thought distracted him. "Can I ask you something?"

"Sure," Sangster said.

"Why did you want Vienna to come to this meeting?"

Vienna looked at him angrily. "*They* wanted me to

come? They summoned me and you were the delivery boy?"

"Well, they asked *me* to come, too," Alex said. He saw her disappointment and felt his face grow hot. "I thought—I thought you liked the ride," he said stupidly.

Professor Montrose leaned forward. "That scarf around your neck is the curse, is it not?"

She looked down, shifting her shoulders so that it danced slightly as if alive—which, Alex now knew, it was. "Yes."

"We will find a cure for you," the professor said. "If you'll let us try."

Sangster interjected, "And if you'll let us keep the scarf after we manage to remove the curse."

Vienna's eyes were wide in something like disbelief. Alex jumped in. "Come on, you can't make a bargain like that. Removing that thing is dangerous. The deal has to be that you make sure it doesn't hurt her in the process."

Sangster threw Montrose a look that said, *See? He's smart.* "What kind of people do you think we are?"

"I'm just sayin'," Alex said.

Vienna ran her fingers along the scarf. "Don't listen to him; if you can cure me, you can keep it."

"It will take some time," Montrose said, "but now

that I'm here and the lab is being set up, we *have* time."

Alex realized that Vienna's curse removal project likely meant he would be giving her frequent rides to the HQ.

I can handle that. But as Alex and Vienna rode back to town, there was a far-off buzzing in his head—not static, not magic, but something more personal and instinctive, as though he were missing something important.

Or maybe he was just afraid of having to wear a tuxedo.

Chapter 25

The next day was finally Friday. Alex, Paul, and Sid brought their clothes to the still-unoccupied New Aubrey House to get ready for the benefit ball, because it was awkward changing and swinging their arms around in the sheeted Kingdom of Cots. Alex would be accompanying Vienna, but Sid wasn't off the hook: He'd be escorting a deb whose date had left Glenarvon in the wake of withdrawals.

In the drawing room they chose for getting changed, a massive mirror hung from wires, threatening to fall and crush them like vested insects. Alex worked on his tie and looked into the mirror at Sid, who had finished his.

"You look like Dracula," Alex said. "A red-haired Dracula."

Sid laughed. "First, Dracula bore no reflection." He fiddled with his own tie. "Second, the whole opera attire thing was a detail that was added in the play."

Alex tore his tie off, starting again, coming closer to the giant mirror. "Why's that?"

"Because it looks *cool*," Paul said. "Good lord, mate, let me before you ruin it." Paul grabbed Alex's tie, curving the fabric up and about in an incomprehensible flurry. He turned Alex back around to face the mirror. "See?"

The finishing piece was something that had been delivered to Alex that morning, a gift from his father, which arrived with the rented tuxedos from Secheron. It was a silver lapel pin, with a discreet *VH* inlaid. A note inside said simply, *Love, Dad.*

Alex swiveled the pin until he was satisfied it was straight. The three boys stood there in front of the mirror, suddenly nervous.

"I feel like The Three Tenors here," Alex said.

"Yeah, this is kinda sad." Sid nodded. "Let's go."

They walked over to the library, where before the crackling fire stood Minhi, Vienna, and a girl Alex immediately recognized as the yodeler from the first

Pumpkin Show, and, though he wasn't totally positive, one of the girls from the woods. She was a junior deb as well and had persuaded Sid to be her escort through tenacious force of will.

Minhi was wearing a blue evening gown that wrapped in a way suggesting an Indian sari. Alex nearly gasped aloud and had to stop himself, feeling his eyes widen. He saw Paul almost stagger when he saw how glamorous she looked.

Vienna was not so dramatically transformed; she had gone from elegant casual to elegant evening, wearing black that went all the way up to her neck, with the green scarf blazing as always.

They seemed absurdly gorgeous and grown-up, and Alex felt strange and unformed in comparison. It occurred to him at that moment that the men wear black and white because they are essentially intended to be invisible next to the women in the gowns.

"Oh my God," said Minhi, laughing as she beheld the boys. "You look like The Three Tenors."

Alex threw up his hands. "Thank you, that is *totally* what I . . ."

"I think you look marvelous," said Vienna, moving forward to touch and peer at Alex's tie. "That's a fantastic knot."

"Thank you. Or thank Paul; he did the knot, you know. I will stop talking now." Alex looked at the girl next to Minhi. "I'm sorry, I don't know your name. . . ."

"Ilsa Applebaum," she said.

Sid said, "Ilsa's dad is, like, the minister of finance for Germany or something."

"Or something?" Ilsa smirked. "Deputy Minister of Finance, Banking Regulation."

Sid turned. "And yet she wants me to be her escort."

"That *is* truly something," Paul said.

Out of the doors of New Aubrey, the procession of six reached the courtyard. Alex saw others heading to the gate and its line of waiting limos as the sun dropped over the trees and the lake.

Vienna walked close to him, and Alex heard her murmuring something in Spanish.

"What's that?" he asked, curious.

"Just a little song my brother used to sing," she said.

"Ours is the Lincoln," Minhi said, as they began to mix with the other couples walking through the gate. She pointed down a long line of vehicles and Alex saw a stretch town car about four cars down. They headed toward it. Alex's phone buzzed. He stopped and took it out. Vienna stopped, too.

"What is it?"

"Text." The caller ID showed up as POLI HQ. That was new; usually it came in as FHOUSE. But whatever. Alex opened it impatiently,

NEEDED NOW. VAN COMING FOR YOU. BACK GATE.

Panicked, Alex looked at the others, who had paused as well.

Paul was eyeing him with concern. "Oh, bloody hell."

"I . . ." Alex slumped. *You've got to be kidding.*

Vienna came around to look him in the eyes. "What's going on?"

"They want me to go."

"What? No, you can't."

"Tell them no, Alex," Minhi said. "That's completely not cool."

Alex heard Ilsa whisper a question to Sid and the boy shrugged.

Another text buzzed.

EMERGENCY.

Alex shook his head, feeling himself separate even before he knew what he had decided. "It's why I'm here," he said.

"It's why you're *here*?" Vienna hissed. "Not tonight, it isn't, for heaven's sake."

Alex pleaded, "Look, I'm sorry."

"Alex!" He was doing something terrible. She needed an escort, at the very least. She couldn't go stag.

"Maybe somebody can lead you—"

A stoic sadness crept into her eyes and she said, *"Eh."*

"Look, I'll try to catch up," Alex said to them all. "It's an emergency."

Paul and Sid shrugged. Minhi just looked mournful. Vienna had already transitioned to controlling the fist of death, and Ilsa was thankfully clueless. He couldn't look at them anymore. Turning, he bolted through the gate and headed clear around the campus to the back. He had barely gotten there when a black van roared around a corner. He felt overwhelmed with anger; it was buzzing in his brain, drowning out every other sensation, and urging him to scream and punch the first person he saw. *Is this my life now? I said I wanted it, so is this what my life is?*

Alex couldn't see through the driver's side window but he started yelling anyway. "What the *hell*, Sangster!" He didn't have a go package, so they'd better have equipment. What was it going to be now? Were they going bungee jumping over another train?

He thrust his phone forward. "You totally destroy my evening with a *text*?"

The van doors slid open.

Steven Merrill grabbed Alex's hand and crushed the cell phone in it like an aluminum can as he yanked him inside. Alex's sliced palm sang with pain. He flew through the air and crashed against the far side of the van.

He rolled to a stop under the grinning, fanged visage of Steven's brother, Bill.

Chapter 26

The Merrills are vampires, thought Alex wildly.

No time for that now. Get the hell out.

Alex scrambled to his feet as he felt the van lurch and begin to accelerate. For a moment he considered leaping away from Bill, who was slowly turning toward him, regarding him as a cat would a wounded mouse. Alex glanced at the front of the van. Maybe he could take the wheel—but no. There was a roll cage installed, heavy mesh, a single window with metal slats showing him the road outside, which was moonlit. The vampires were driving with no lights.

"Look at you!" Bill said, his face pale, his eyes dilated and icy. "You look like Dracula."

"Dracula didn't wear a tux," Alex recited, backing into the rear corner, grasping for the door handle. If he opened it now he might be able to escape. He'd have to roll, and it wouldn't be pretty on him or his tuxedo. His hand reached the silver handle and he gave it a yank. For a second it was jammed and he felt the brothers at his back, the static hissing in his brain, and then the handle jerked free and turned. The doors flew open and he grabbed the top of the van, watching the lines on the road whiz by into darkness.

Go. He could do it, just leap, keep his arms over his face. He'd break his elbows, probably. That would hurt. *Go.* The books his father had given him told him about survival in cases like this and the one piece of advice he could count on was that you had to *accept that there will be pain.* Pain doesn't kill. Pain just hurts. *So go.*

Damn, that was gonna hurt.

"No, no," said Bill, sounding amused, and as Alex looked back he saw the boy nod at Steven, who leapt like a tiger and snatched him again, sharp claws digging into his collar. He hurled Alex in a second time and Alex felt himself roll along the roof and slam into the mesh cage before crumpling to the floor.

The force shook the van and sent Alex's head spinning; the van careened for a second and kept moving.

The driver, wearing a fetching black cap in the darkness, did not look back.

"Why would you do this?!" Alex roared. Steven took a seat at the bench chair and his attention was caught for a moment by a piece of felt that had been torn from the ceiling as Alex had crashed along it. He clawed at it slowly, as if amazed at the sharpness of his newly reinvigorated nails. *So sharp, it cuts anything! Even felt!*

Bill slammed the doors shut and came to sit next to his brother. "Did he ask something?"

Alex couldn't believe they would do this to themselves. Sid had laid out the process: The bite was poison, so poisonous it could kill you, so powerful it could save the dead. If you died and the spinal cord was intact—and you hadn't had embalming fluid interrupt the vampirism process—you were in the clear, ready to go, *come on back and bite some people.*

But it did things to you. It made you colder, it ate away at the part of your brain that gave you empathy, the better to be a killing machine. But who would want this for themselves? "I asked, *how could you do this*?" Alex repeated.

"Do what?"

Part of Alex's question was borne of sheer need to keep them engaged before they decided to rip him apart.

He was trapped in a van with a pair of vampires, newborn or no.

The van turned a corner. Oh, and they were taking him somewhere, so if they didn't rip him apart now, what they were headed for couldn't be good. He had an idea, though. Chances are they were going straight down to the Scholomance, and he had escaped from that place once, and once was enough. *Think. Get out. How?*

But the question was also borne of a horror—the person he was looking at, Bill Merrill, wasn't supposed to be dead. His brother, Steven, wasn't supposed to be dead. This wasn't how it worked; you didn't just wake up one day and decide to commit suicide by vampire.

"Bill, you're a jerk. You're the biggest freaking jerk I've ever met. *Ever,* and I have some experience. But one thing I know is that jerks look out for themselves. And you've thrown it *all away*!"

"That's interesting," said Bill. "That you would suddenly care so much about me. That's really sweet."

Steven raised a hand. "*I* haven't thrown anything away."

Bill leaned forward, his pale face glistening in the dim moonlight that shot through the darkened windows. "Let me ask you something. What do *you* know about any of it? You don't know *jack.* I've been going to school with you for a month and a half, and I don't think you've ever asked a thing about me."

Oh dear Lord, I've hurt Bill Merrill's feelings. The very idea was absurd. "You made my life miserable!" Alex cried.

Steven raised a hand.

"Him too," Alex said. "So don't give me that crap about how much you were secretly hoping I was going to pull you both aside and trade baseball cards with you."

"I'm just saying that you don't know a damn thing," Bill responded. The smile had gone away. "It's easy for you, isn't it? Three Americans, the three of us, and, buddy, you have some behavioral issues, but I see you, and it's easy. You got this way, this walk, this smarm, this confidence. Everybody *likes* you," he said, licking the *l* hard against razor-sharp teeth. "Not like us."

Alex was flabbergasted. "I'm not going to make you feel better about yourself, you *maniac*; you are a freaking *vampire* now."

"Listen, buddy," Bill said. "I got one thing in this world. One thing. And that's him." Steven pursed his lips in acknowledgment. Bill went on, "There wasn't gonna be anything left after he was gone. Do you get that? Is that even possible for you to understand?"

"I . . ." Alex was trying to get a handle on this suddenly

confessional Bill. "Bill, you were alive. People die in accidents. You have *parents*, they—"

"They NEVER CAME," Bill shouted. "Steven was in the hospital and they couldn't be bothered to come. They wouldn't even take my calls. Not. One. Word."

"But you were transferred out," Alex said.

"That was our *new* family," Bill said. "They made us an offer. It was an offer Steven needed. But it was one I wanted."

"Oh, man." Alex shook his head. "You poor fool, this life isn't gonna be what you think. You're gonna have to kill. You're gonna leave everything you've ever known behind."

The window to the front of the van shot open and a female voice said, "Somehow I think they can handle that."

Sound of wheels on gravel. The van was slowing and Alex instantly rose, jumping once more for the rear door. But Bill grabbed him and held his arms behind his back.

As the van came to a stop, the driver removed her hat. Alex saw Elle look back through the grating. "Put him out."

Steven came from nowhere with a fierce punch to the side of Alex's head, and all went dark.

Chapter 27

"One freaking drop," came the voice from the haze. He blinked his eyes and felt the sting of his contact lenses, swiveling them around. His head was singing like crazy, and the voice of Elle boomed in it and reverberated with the concussive echo of Steven's blow. Vampire could throw a sucker punch.

"One . . . freaking . . . drop!" came the voice again, screaming this time, and he shook fully awake, aware that she was screaming in his ear before he saw her there.

"Oh, Elle, you'll be the death of me," Alex said, so close that he could smell the strange mixture of death and mint that vampires all seemed to have for breath. He looked past her and saw a giant cloth wall stretching up endlessly, a sheet. He'd spent so much time surrounded by sheets lately, but this was an industrial kind, probably made of heavy wool and wax.

His arms were above his head, Alex realized, and he looked up to see that they were tied together with rope. The rope extended up to some sort of hinged boom or crane, fifteen feet above his head. Then he looked down.

He was twenty feet off the ground, his feet barely touching an iron beam. Below, he saw a wooden pier, and black water lapping against it. The water extended a hundred yards across to another pier.

He was in a boatyard of some kind, for building and fixing boats and rolling them back out onto the lake. Down below, on the dock, the Merrill brothers waited, watching as Elle continued haranguing him from her perch on the iron beam next to him.

She had gotten rid of the leather coat and was wearing Scholomance whites, with tight leggings and little white leather boots, and a tight wrap around her body that ended in a pulled-back hood. "If you hadn't shed that one drop, we'd be *done* by now."

"What are you talking about?" he asked honestly.

"I'm talking about *Claire,*" Elle said. "It was all supposed to happen that night. She'd be back to lead us—to lead *me.* And I was *ready* for that."

Alex blinked against the sweat on his brow, feeling some of it stream into his eyes. He blinked as it swished around, threatening to unseat his contacts. "The skull-headed lady?"

"The new queen is not a skull-headed lady," Elle said, eyes blazing. "That was just her way in. And she needed blood. And she got some—from you. And then, you little insect, you got away before she could finish."

Alex lost his footing for a second and sank with the rope before finding it again. Yes, okay. He had it now. That night at the Villa Diodati, Icemaker *had* cut him, briefly. The cut on his neck that had taken a few weeks to heal. "Elle, I have no idea what you're talking about. Icemaker *barely* cut me."

"One drop," she repeated.

It was possible. He thought back, forcing himself back to the night in the cellar, the skeletal form behind the veil. Icemaker had lifted him up with one strong arm and put a sharp fingernail to his neck, hissing, "She needs more blood." And he'd cut. And then Paul had arrived.

Hey, Paul, now would be a good time.

"Blood is blood, isn't it?" Alex said. "Right?" But of course not. Or else Elle wouldn't be this bonkers about it.

"Oh, I'm afraid not," Elle said. "Once you were part

of the sacrifice it had to be you that finished it. I had to haul the queen back to the Scholomance myself and hide her away like a *doll* because she wasn't done yet."

"Ahhhh," Alex said, staring into her insane eyes. "That's what you wanted my blood for. That's why you sent the Glimmerhook, to suck it up."

"As long as you *died* it was supposed to be fine. The Scholomance would have been happy, and I would have your blood."

Alex looked around. "I don't see any resurrected queens here. Well, there're the Merrills."

"Hey!" Bill shouted.

"You're gonna love working with him," Alex said to Elle.

"I'm not taking you down to *her*," Elle said. "The administration won't allow it; they've completely lost interest in resurrecting Claire."

This was what Sangster had heard about the Scholomance. The project for Claire had been canceled. Because they didn't have the blood they needed, and they'd moved on.

"Maybe she's not a queen, Elle," said Alex with a hint of desperation. He glanced at Elle's stance. Maybe he could kick her. But she was firmly rooted and it would have to be a perfect shot. "I mean, Claire was just a girl that Icemaker wanted to rule with. She wasn't that special."

"Liar!" she screamed.

Alex studied her face, the blue blood within raging underneath the skin at her forehead. "What do you care? You're a psychopath by nature and she's not a queen."

"Where'd you learn that, from a book? What do you know about Claire?"

"I actually get this secondhand, but there's a guy who knows everything about it all and if you cut me down, I can go get him."

"No, I'll just take the blood," she said. She drew a dagger from her belt.

Alex eyed the blade, long and silver, like the ones she had given to the girls in the woods. She spun it in her fingers and he watched the muscles in her alabaster forearm ripple.

This is bad. Ask the questions.

What's going on?

I'm tied up. She's gonna cut me.

What do you have?

I have myself.

He kicked out at her and Elle zipped away, then slashed out, slicing through the cloth of his tuxedo and sending three ridiculously expensive pearl buttons into the deep.

"Hey! Shouldn't you be out trying to catch Montrose again? I thought you and Ultravox were busy with that."

"Montrose?" She snorted. "You think we brought in a player like Ultravox over *Chatterbox*? You morons really are full of yourselves. You can snoop all you want, Alex. You can't keep up with us. Ultravox has bigger fish to fry."

"But—" Alex said, realizing he sounded completely taken aback. *Get that under control, think, think.*

Stickiness as blood began to ooze from the shallow cut. God, that stung. He worked his hands and felt the icy tingle of them going numb. *Bigger fish to fry. Because he's an assassin. He's still here and he's got bigger fish, bigger than scientists. Bigger like politicians.*

"The ball," Alex spat, suddenly realizing it. The ball would be full of visiting dignitaries, all on a boat with their teenage children—many of whom had already been programmed to kill. "He's here to stop the treaty, the information treaty."

"And you missed it." Elle clicked her tongue.

"But why do vampires care about an information-sharing treaty?"

"Oh, Al, I swear when people start talking about

treaties I want to shave my own head with a cheese grater," Elle said. "Now where were we?"

Alex tried to stall her. "You gonna spill nine pints all over the dock?"

Her nostrils flared for a moment as she caught the scent of his blood. Her eyes took on a sensuous look and she spun the knife again. "Nope."

"You can't waste it."

"Bring out the bowl," called Elle.

Down below, the Merrills pulled the blanket off a stand that looked like a generator, but now he saw was a rolling table with an enormous white collecting bowl.

"Ah, another bird feeder." They rolled the bowl down the dock, a couple of vampiric Vanna Whites, the lovely assistants of Elle the vampire. They brought it to a stop below him and worked together to line it up. They seemed to take a moment disagreeing over where it would be perfectly plumb.

Not good. Dammit, *what do you have?*

"Merrills!"

They looked at him, satisfied with the placement of the bowl. "I think that's it," said Bill.

Think. Steven was injured. Nobody came.

"Seriously, you couldn't get through on the phone?

That sucks," Alex said.

"People are bound to disappoint," Bill said evenly.

Alex looked at Elle. "You guys sent the withdrawal papers?"

"We take care of our own," Elle said.

"And so how did you block Bill's calls?"

Elle blinked. "What?"

"It's a lie, Bill," Alex cried. "You listening?"

"Shut up. Come on, boss, let's drain this guy."

"Oh my God, you're such a chump," Alex said, nearly delirious, as Elle tried to decide whether to cut him open from stem to stern or start with a throat cut. "Bill, get real, your parents didn't abandon you. She *blocked your calls.* She wanted a couple of simpleminded Igors she could boss around and you fit the pattern."

Steven looked up and spoke, finally. "Why would you say that?"

"Because I saw a *care package* for you *from your parents* stuffed into the garbage at the hospital," Alex rasped as Elle brought the knife close.

"That's it," Elle said, bringing the dagger back for the swing.

"She made sure you wouldn't get it so you'd do this," Alex shouted.

Down came the knife. Alex closed his eyes.

Something heavy landed on the beam. It was Bill, pushing Alex to the side. Alex swung wild into the air on the boom, spinning.

"Is this true?" Bill was saying.

"Hey . . ."

"Is that *true*?" he cried.

Alex yanked on the rope and screamed as it bit into his wrists, whipping his body once, twice, and then finally he was head over heels, wrapping his ankles around the rope. He let the rope dig into his ankles, some of the weight coming off his hands. He nearly screamed with relief as blood began to flow through his wrists again.

Elle put her hand on Bill's face. "Hey, this is all just the beginning."

"I threw away everything for you," he cried, pushing her furiously. Elle fell back off the beam and sailed through the air.

Still hanging upside down, Alex heard Elle land in the water as he began to untie the knotted rope around his hands with his teeth. After a moment his hands came free and he grabbed the rope, letting his legs whip down until he hung by his hands, which were aching but getting their feeling back.

Elle climbed onto the dock, pointing at him. "Don't let him—"

And Steven smashed her in the back of the head with the bowl.

She leapt at Steven as Bill closed in and Alex swung once more. He let go and suddenly there was nothing but air. Alex took a hard gulp.

Then cold. He plunged deep, forcing the air from his lungs and sinking fast.

Alex's body sang with cold as he swam, finding the piers and sticking to them, not daring to come up until he had gone at least fifty yards.

When he emerged under the dock, he heard screaming, and a vampire battle royale. He climbed up on the dock and ran, not looking back to see who would win.

Chapter 28

The Secheron marina was alive with Friday night activity, partiers and diners out walking up and down the giant pier. Alex followed the bright lights, his tux dripping wet, scanning for his next move. He was running out of time.

On the water, down the rippling black surface of the lake, Alex made out a large craft, a cruise ship that would have been small at sea but was massive for even a long lake like Geneva. He could see the lights up and down its body. That was the cruise ship *Allimarc.* His friends were there, and Alex was on a dock with nothing but seafood and martinis at hand.

He needed a boat, something with power, but the clanging of the lines against the poles along the marina taunted him with nothing but sailboats. That would be nice any other day, even if he could remember the knots, but it wouldn't do now. Then he reached a watercraft rental shop, long lines of Jet Skis and Sea-Doos tied up. Closed?

No, maybe not—he heard keys jingling at a side door of a shack between two thin jetties where the craft were unlocked and rented. A man in white pants with a black T-shirt was locking up. Alex could rent one.

Alex started to move toward the man, reaching into his pockets for his wallet. But of course it was gone, because Nothing. Could ever be. Easy.

Beg for a Sea-Doo?

An attractive girl in a yachting cap came around the shack and put her arm on the rental manager, a girlfriend, probably. She was eager to get up the big pier to the restaurant.

"Hey!" Alex shouted, but the guy didn't hear him over the wind coming off the lake.

Just then another sound came, the chugging of one last craft, a yellow WaveRunner, with a pair of university-age kids on it, drunk and whipping wildly as they brought the craft toward the jetty. They were late, obviously.

The rental manager was talking to his girl and Alex ran up the pier, out to the edge, sliding on his slick shoes to a stop at the end of the thin pier. He waved at the pair.

"Had enough?" Alex shouted in French, smiling like an idiot. *Come on. Give your WaveRunner to the nice boy in the tuxedo.*

They came to a stop by the pier. "Don't we have to take it all the way?" the boy answered.

"No, no, it's okay," Alex said. He gestured for them to come alongside the ladder that went down from the end of the jetty. He dared to glance back at the manager, who had now stopped making time with the girl and was turning his attention up the jetty.

Alex offered his hand and the guy grabbed it, merrily climbing the ladder. He started shouting about what a great time he'd had, or something, all of it fast and Italian and Alex wasn't listening because he was reaching his hand for the girl. She grabbed it, laughed and shrieked, and fell back.

"Come on," he called as genially as he could. *Come on, for the love of all that's holy, get your drunk ass off the WaveRunner.*

She took his hand once more and put a bare foot on the ladder. For a second he thought she was going to lose it again but she climbed this time, and as she found herself on the dock, Alex heard the manager calling. "*Attendez!*"

Alex jumped on the craft, feeling it slosh down into

the water with his weight. He twisted the throttle and stood still.

It was off. The guy had taken out the key when he climbed off.

The manager was coming fast now.

"Hey, I need the key!" Alex shouted to the Italian, who looked confused for a second, with good reason. Alex waved his hand at the manager, then pointed at the enormous blue float in the guy's hand. Hanging off the float was a telephone cord and a large metal ignition key. "I gotta take it to him, gimme the key!"

The guy jauntily saluted and tossed Alex the key as the manager arrived, running full bore. Alex slapped the key into the ignition and turned it, feeling the motor rev to life, churning in the water.

"Don't worry," he shouted as he gunned the engine. Alex looked back as the jetty shrank in the distance, the manager's wails of protest disappearing in the wind. Water was roaring up from the rear of the watercraft, and he picked up speed, standing tall and leaning forward, the craft bouncing high on the waves.

Soon the darkness of the water gave way to a crazy quilt of colored reflection. Ahead of him loomed the massive waterborne hulk where Ultravox was ready to make his final move.

Chapter 29

Anyone on the promenade deck who cared to look might have picked out the bright yellow WaveRunner approaching at a steady clip, but no one did. As he got closer, Alex heard calypso music streaming from above. There were teens and adults on the deck, arm in arm, looking at one another more than at the dark water.

Alex came up along the starboard side, hugging the side of the ship, scanning the white metal for any kind of access. The water was churning and he had to keep about two yards away to avoid getting swamped and sucked under. The ship was not moving fast, but it was kicking up a dangerous spray.

The *Allimarc* was not as large as a typical cruise

ship—it was more of a giant yacht—but for a landlocked (if enormous) lake, the ship made a fantastically opulent statement. It was clearly very new, and Alex felt certain it would be outfitted with every geegaw a self-impressed ship owner would want, from HD screens in every stateroom to marine compactors for recycling glass and aluminum waste down to handy little blocks, to water purifiers to bring in lake water for use in cooking. Like the cars they were driven in, the ship was a symbol of the power of the parents of these schools' students. The students themselves might be just kids, the ship was saying, but we the parents are powerful, even dangerous.

As he came around the curve of the hull he saw that the *Allimarc* had a rescue ladder near the prow, going all the way down under the waterline, cutting its own groove in the lake. Alex came up alongside, letting go of the WaveRunner, and grabbed on to the ladder. The WaveRunner whipped past his feet as he scrambled up. He heard a heavy, chunky sound as the yellow craft got caught up in the churn and disappeared beneath the ship, and Alex mentally apologized to the rental manager. The Polidorium could replace it.

Xylophone music accompanied him up the ladder. When he reached the top, he peered over the edge, keeping his head behind a huge life preserver and stanchion.

The deck at the prow was deserted. Alex scanned, seeing the lights of the bridge up above, and the tops of a few crewmen's heads. No static. He grabbed the side and climbed, dropping onto the deck. As he hit the boards his dress shoes slid and he tumbled, crying out briefly as he fell in a mound of thick blue rope.

Alex stood up, breathing, taking in the calypso music and the cold wind leaching body heat through his jacket. He was dripping water. Okay. Now what?

The music shifted to a more orchestral number—a live orchestra, he could tell. Alex slunk along the deck, sticking to the bulkhead. The promenade, where the air-seeking partygoers were gathered, was above—he had to stay close in, to avoid being seen.

A pair of adults came around a corner up ahead. Instinctively Alex waved and they waved back. He saw a door and ducked through it.

The jangling, oscillating chirps and trills of a casino drowned out any hint of the orchestra from the ballroom above. Alex moved through the darkened, smoky cave, waving off the stale cigarette smoke, past a few more adults enrapt by the charms of the slot machines. Amazing that some parents would come all this way to see their kids, but would probably spend the next six hours right here, tugging at the golden arm.

Alex exited the casino and found himself at the center of the ship, facing a huge stairwell with brass railings and gilt-edged rugs and thankfully a guide plaque on the wall. This was level 1, and the ballroom was on 3, one up from the promenade deck.

Soaking or not, he had to just *go*. Alex ran his hands through his wet hair, slicking it back.

Two flights up he found a sign: MINISTERS BALL AND BENEFIT. As if there were anything else going on.

A woman was speaking, and the voice sounded full but older, probably in her sixties.

". . . a tribute to these fine young people that they have weathered these events so well. Even now, a house is being refurbished where Glenarvon will continue its work. But that's not all: There is much more work to be done on the school's own grounds. This is why . . ."

Alex headed out onto the walk around the ballroom, taking his place next to some plants and peering in.

How was it going to work? In the woods, Elle had played Ultravox's voice, and that had been the cue. But how would they do it here? There was a PA system, of course. Should he go look for the PA?

In the ballroom the speech subsided, and Alex saw another staircase, leading up to a dining area. There was a crowd gathered up above, and he could see boys in tuxes and the girls in evening gowns. There was a woman, gray haired, elegant, in a head-to-toe sequined gown, standing next to a microphone with a stack of large, black index cards.

"And now the moment you've all been waiting for: our debuts," the woman said.

The attendees of the ball had gathered along the edges, and the woman began reading names.

"Miss Millicent Deveraux." Alex saw a stunning seventeen-year-old come forward, at the hand of a gentleman in a tux. He stepped forward and handed her off to her escort as the woman went into Miss Millicent's many swell-sounding accomplishments. Apparently wintered in the Alps, where she was teaching ice sculpture on the side. Did they make this stuff up?

Alex caught a glimmer of green in the waiting room above—Vienna. She was standing next to a man who must be Mr. Cazorla.

And there was Minhi—next to a tall, olive-skinned woman who looked like her, but with a pixie cut and a little more fullness. And now as he scanned he saw the rest—Ilsa behind them, Paul and Sid, waiting in the wings, and next to them a boy Paul was talking to. Javi, the RA from school. An escort in a pinch for Vienna. They both spoke Spanish. What luck.

The wet coat was bulky and annoying and he stripped it off, letting it fall at his feet, his lapel pin clacking on the boards.

The woman announced that each debutante would be met with a gift, a pen—a gleaming platinum Montblanc, in fact, commemorating the upcoming international meeting this ball was intended to kick off. Although of course Glenarvon was accepting offers of support, Alex figured that one of those pens could pay for most of the books in the library. *What are you doing, Alex? You're here on a hunch. You should be here for real. You should be up there. The mission was a fake and Elle was just playing along when you stretched it out into a threat against the ball. You're as much a chump as the Merrills.*

He thought all of this with a blistering honesty. No, wait. He *thought* that he thought that.

The man standing behind him had said it.

Alex felt static, finally, far away and muffled.

"Let's take a walk, Alex," said Ultravox. "There's something you'll want to do."

Chapter 30

Minhi received her Montblanc from Paul and held on to it as she took his hand and they stepped down the rest of the stairs.

They began to dance as the announcements went on, and she watched the crowd. Her mom was on the side, talking to Mr. Otranto, and she was nodding in a way Minhi had seen before: It was the serene look of a woman hearing a pitch. There were stations around the ballroom where people gathered for fun or for paying a lot of money. Not far from the bar near a side door, there was a table where Ms. Daughtry was taking pledges for the rebuilding of Glenarvon. The punch bowl (for the students) was on the other side of the room where a representative from the upcoming Ministers' Conference was working the same angle. Minhi's mom would stop at one or the other soon, probably just to shut Otranto up.

The orchestra segued into calypso again. Javi and Vienna came into view over Paul's shoulder, Vienna looking charming, smiling as any deb should, but not all the way to her eyes. "You have to admit, this is better than the cages down in the Scholomance," Paul said.

Minhi laughed. They were swaying, dancing about as much as Paul could manage. "And I got a pen," she said.

She dropped the pen into her tiny handbag before taking his hand again. That was better.

"What?" Paul asked, looking at her.

"Just . . . enjoying the music," she said. The dancing was to go on for a few numbers and then there would be a switch; the hostess would announce that they should each dance with their parents, which was charming except that Minhi was there with her mom and she wasn't sure if they could just sit it out or decide who should lead.

"Damn cell phone," she said aloud, not intending to.

"Yeah," Paul said as kindly as he could. He looked around. "You want me to get you some punch?"

She smiled. "Sure."

Paul gallantly bowed and she curtsied, and he was off, showing some measure of relief. None of this felt quite right.

For a moment she did listen to the music, the rhythmic xylophones and bongos thrumming in her head. She turned around and looked at Ms. Daughtry, who smiled back and waved.

Behind Ms. Daughtry she saw a glint of metal on the floor, shimmering like a jewel in a mound of dark cloth. She waited for Paul and studied the ballroom banners for a moment.

She shot her eyes back to the glint.

Minhi found herself walking toward it and coming around the open doorway, staring at the jewel. Her heart began to thump against her chest as she knelt, reaching out to touch a soaking tuxedo jacket that had been tossed on the floor, water streaming around it.

It was Alex's lapel pin.

Minhi stood up as the hostess started to announce the parental dance. She followed the stream of water with her eyes and began to run.

"You've done very well," said Ultravox, who still wore a peasant shirt and casual pants, no slave to fashion. Down in the bowels of the ship, in a hold about the size of a two-car garage, the man's voice echoed off metal walls as they strolled past pallets of cardboard and bins of glass and aluminum. They were walking through a hold where trash and recyclables would be processed, Alex dimly realized. Then the realization drifted away.

"You're probably wondering why I don't have an army," Ultravox said. "The Scholomance is so obsessed with making its point with droves of soldiers, but I find a little bit of leadership can go a long way."

The vampire was just behind Alex and to the side. Alex started to break free of the voice, when Ultravox said again, "No, you don't want to raise your hands. You're tired of all that. Look what it's got you."

They were approaching an open door at the end of the room. For a moment it looked strange and unfamiliar, and then Alex blinked and saw that it was a bunk, not full-size, but the kind you'd find on the train from Munich to Rome, decent enough to doze for a few hours after you've been walking all day. Ultravox's voice went on, outside yet somehow inside his head.

"Alex, I told you before that this was as good as it's going to get, but you've only made it worse. Isn't that just terrible? You have all of these opportunities around you, but you'll bungle them. The young ladies around you, you can't seem to decide what to do about them. And I'll tell you," the man with the scratchy face and liquid voice continued, "that's really just as well. You can believe that you would have found happiness, but most people don't. You won't; at this rate you'll be a slave to what you really want to be doing, running around playing cops and robbers. It's not going to get any better, and it will only get worse. But that's all right. Tomorrow you can think about it some more."

Ultravox came around and patted him firmly on the shoulder. "What you want to do now is get some rest."

It was true. Ultravox was working for the Scholomance but you had to hand it to the guy, what he said always made sense. Alex had allowed Steven to be hurt, had allowed both Merrills to become vampires. He hadn't prevented his school from burning up. He had disappointed his friends tonight, and for what? There wasn't any stopping beings that were always going to be stronger and smarter and . . .

Ultravox stepped ahead of him and reached into the bunk. A block of shiny metal sat on the bed, and then as Ultravox spoke Alex realized he had been wrong. "Someone left some bedding here," said Ultravox. The block of metal shimmered and Alex blinked, and it was just a pile of blankets and pillows. "Let me get it out of the way."

Ultravox picked up the bedding and set it aside—Alex saw it shimmer, flashing with metal and then smoothing over again—and the vampire put his hands in his cotton pockets.

"It's a universal feeling, you know. We all ruin our lives in our own ways. I myself had the greatest voice ever known, and I squandered it quietly, living in the shadows. Letting people like Icemaker take all the glory, letting people like your various relatives—few of whom were nearly as resourceful as you, by the way—disrupt any little plan I had going. Your family has certainly been . . . a constant joy, to me and to the Scholomance.

"Six months ago I was offered the ball project. Big targets, and a noble cause. The Scholomance didn't want the treaty and they knew I'd be the best choice for finding a way to eliminate the key players. And this will come to pass. But a month ago, the richest target of all came along: another Van Helsing. An active one." The vampire came closer and spoke in his ear. "I can do with my voice what Icemaker couldn't do with an army of thousands: eliminate you. The Scholomance will have no choice but to finally give me the recognition and authority I deserve."

Ultravox patted Alex on the shoulder. "Bury all that

now. Rest," he said. "Your limbs are heavy and none of it matters anyway."

The mellifluous voice dripped through Alex's body, moving him, of course. He stepped forward, grabbed the inside of the bunk, and hauled himself up, lying down. He wanted to sleep. Otherwise he would just keep thinking about how it wasn't going to get any better.

"I had heard that you might be the exception," Ultravox was saying. "The only one of your family in generations who had that extra something that your ancestor and his mad son had. But no, you're just another adventurer, like your father. Not unimpressive—but hardly my problem." He sighed. "If you think about your life, you will see a fog crossing, enveloping you. It's better in the fog, where you can rest, and all of this goes away. It should be just a moment."

Alex barely heard Ultravox say, as he was walking away, "Good night, Van Helsing."

Chapter 31

In the ballroom Paul returned from the punch bowl to find a blank space where Minhi had been standing.

He kept his chin up—not one to go about slouching was Paul—but he had to admit this date was going poorly.

"Is that champagne?" Vienna spoke, and Paul looked up to see her standing with her father, who was the *ministro de* something or other.

Paul held out one of the glasses. "It's, ah, sparkling . . . fruity something or other."

She took the glass. "And to think the crystal is Lalique," she said. "This just seems wrong."

Vienna's father was round at the middle and

mustachioed, and he could have passed either for an aged matinee idol or a mustache-twirling cartoon villain. Paul turned to him and offered the other glass. "Care for one?"

"Sparkly fruity something or other?" said the man, with the same accent as Vienna's. "No, that's for recovering alcoholics and teenagers."

"Wouldn't care to live like a teen?" Paul smiled.

"Wouldn't care to recover," the Spaniard said. He didn't wink but his mustache sort of danced. "I'm off to find the real thing. Let me know if anything interesting happens."

Minhi's mother approached. "Have you seen Minhi?"

Paul shrugged.

"It's a small ship," Mr. Cazorla said to Minhi's mother. "She can't have gotten far. Join me, I'm looking for something stronger than sparkly fruity something or other."

Minhi's mother rolled her eyes exactly, precisely the way that Minhi often did, and the two of them headed off for the good stuff.

"Where *did* your girlfriend go?" Vienna said, watching the parents wander away.

"Is that what she is?" Paul asked. "I sort of wonder."

"That's a terrible answer," Vienna said. "That's an

American answer; I'd expect that from Alex, not from you." She laughed, and Paul found her teasing very soft edged and infectious.

Vienna went on, "You're supposed to say 'But of course! She is my girlfriend!' Or, 'No, you fool! I would not have her!' Leave the half answers and melancholia to the Americans. And the French. They hate one another but they are alike in those ways."

Paul took a sip of the sparkling whatever and blanched. Syrupy stuff. "I don't know. She wandered off."

"My date wandered off before we got in the car," answered Vienna.

"That's . . ." Paul shook his head, suddenly defensive of Alex. "He can't help that. The bloke's on a short leash." And that was the truth. Alex was always going to be half there. "He's another bloody tennis player."

"A what?"

"Tennis players. Gymnasts, speed skaters, prodigies. The professionals. They look like high school students, they talk like them, but they catch whatever bug, get nabbed by some agent, and you've lost them as a friend, or lost a lot of them. That's what Alex is. Think of him as a speed skater."

"Eh, I look around this room and I will bet the speed

skaters were able to make it," Vienna said. "I think it's absurd. You're only supposed to be married to your work when you have an actual marriage to ruin; when you're fourteen it's simply ridiculous."

"Boy," said Paul, "get a few sparkling ciders in you and you're a Spanish Audrey Hepburn all of a sudden. Where's Javi?"

"Around here somewhere," Vienna said.

"I *love* Audrey Hepburn," said Ilsa as she appeared with Sid in tow. Paul had noticed Sid gamely attempting to keep up with his taller, more graceful date. Not so bad when the band was playing calypso, but when they took a break and the PA started pumping French techno, Sid was lost. "Did you know she grew up in the Netherlands?"

"Who's that?" Sid asked.

"Audrey . . . someone who was never in a vampire movie," Paul said.

Sid looked around. "Where's Minhi?"

Paul and Vienna shrugged, and then the music cut out.

It happened suddenly—one minute the PA system playing an appalling French cover of Rammstein's "Du Hast," and the next the heavy bass and French singing stopped, interrupted by a sudden high-pitched whistle.

"May I have your attention," came a mellifluous voice speaking in English with an untraceable accent. Paul watched as the entire crowd stopped, listening, some in curiosity and some in anger.

"Some of you are prepared for this night. If so, there is something that you will want to do."

Paul looked at Vienna and Sid. "Oh, no."

Most of the crowd was listening to this new voice with complete incredulity, but Paul noticed a subtle shift among a few of them—among the debutantes. The debs had frozen, and appeared to be in full receiver mode next to their parents.

Paul saw a tall chestnut-haired deb step forward, her head lifted toward the sound. Another girl near her, a senior by the look of her, had also tilted her head up, eyes glassy and wide.

They were the same girls who had gone gaga over Sid's stories. They were still poisoned.

"You have in your hands a symbol of your own slavery," said the voice. "It is time to make yourself free."

Suddenly the daughters lashed out with the pens, leaping behind their parents, each bringing one arm around the parent's waist, the other bringing her newly received, sharp-as-a-knife Montblanc pen up to the mother's or father's throat.

"Come with us," said the voice on the intercom.

"Come with us," said the daughters.

Paul saw Vienna running. She grabbed her own father, but she was dragging him away from the others. "I'm sorry," he heard her say. "Hurry, we have to get out of here."

Chapter 32

Alex lay in the bunk, thinking about the night he had spent with his father in the Munich train station as he began to drift to sleep. He shifted his head. He didn't really need anything more than a light pillow, but the one on the bunk was less than ideal. It seemed hardly there.

The words of Ultravox were still looping in his head, repeating in multiple threads of sound, urging him to rest, to sleep, to give up, to let it go.

The words seemed quiet and yet they were so constant that they blocked out everything, even blotting out the thought of the train station in Munich, the thoughts of his family. Every thought that was not still echoing the voice of Ultravox seemed dulled and distant, and it made him tired to think.

Far in the back of Alex's brain, a lion was moaning, quiet and far-off, muffled and blanketed.

Alex felt himself drifting to sleep but his head wasn't perfectly comfortable, the pillow was too thin. Ultravox had picked up some extra bedding and moved it away. Had there been another pillow?

The moaning was rumbling, far-off, like a jackhammer a mile away, a jackhammer he couldn't hear because the millions of whispers of Ultravox drowned out those troublesome sounds.

Jackhammers and lions . . . all the noise . . . Alex's life was made up of noise and conflict and constant movement. But Ultravox had explained to him that there was a better path: sleep. Don't listen to the jackhammer, to the lion.

His head was miserably uncomfortable. He couldn't even accomplish sleeping right. Alex opened his eyes slightly, looking for the stack of bedding Ultravox had set aside.

It sat there on a small table, the stack of blankets and pillows Ultravox had pulled out.

No one can overcome it, Alex. His voice threads the brain with his will, until you can't hear anything else.

In the distance, he heard trees falling and roots being pulled aside. Giant paws slapping earth. Faraway trees in the back of the woods, where the lion growled, barely audible.

The stack of bedding seemed strange and dull. Alex looked at it.

There's something special about you, and it has them worried.

The whispering of Ultravox, the echoes in his head, increased, and for a moment he lost the sound of the falling trees. But suddenly the distant noise was there again, growling and pounding.

The bedding stacked on the table looked strange and shimmering. For a second it changed and Alex saw a block of aluminum cans, pressed by thousands of pounds of force into a perfect and portable block.

Now the sound of the pounding was growing, and Alex saw the bedding and then he blinked on purpose and saw the block, and tried to think.

There was a clicking sound, a machine, and Alex started to feel the bunk vibrating.

The lion—his own brain, his own Alex Van Helsing static—was running desperately toward him, *wake up*, the trees falling with wrenching and tearing sounds, and now Alex did something he had never done before.

He saw the static. He was aware of it, he reached out to it and beckoned to it, and like a lion of legend it burst through and uprooted trees and roared.

The lion roared and Ultravox whispered in his brain until the lion opened its jaws and sucked the whispering wind away.

The bedding was compacted aluminum cans. The bunk was a recycling compactor. He was about to be crushed.

Alex rolled, kicking and falling to the floor as the sides of the compactor began to vibrate louder. In a moment a heavy glass door, like an oven door, dropped over the compactor, and he watched as the two sides slammed together with incredible force, reducing absolutely nothing to jelly.

He nodded to himself, shaken but satisfied. So that was it. Ultravox was a one-man superweapon but Alex had the capacity to resist. That power in his brain that he called the static—it was more powerful than a magic voice. Alex heard footsteps and spun around to see Minhi, running into the hold.

"Alex!"

She leapt into his arms and hugged him for a long moment before pulling away.

"Minhi, what's going on up above?" He was looking

around. He could barely remember the walk down here.

"Nothing," she said. "I found your pin; I thought you were in trouble."

Alex looked at the compactor. "It's all right now. I think I figured some things out."

"Are you all right?" She came closer, looking at him. He realized he was still shaking his head, trying to sift away the last vestiges of the voice of Ultravox.

"I'm fine, sincerely, I'm fine." Then Alex smacked his forehead. "We gotta go. He's gonna kill someone. Come on." He started to run for the stairs.

"Sometimes I can't believe you," Minhi said, running after him.

"I told you I'd catch up," Alex answered as they bounded up the stairs together.

CHAPTER 33

By the time they had climbed up three flights to the promenade deck, Alex and Minhi could hear a new sound—a warbling, hissing voice playing over the orchestra in the ballroom.

Alex stopped, holding up a hand.

"What?" Minhi asked.

"Minhi, you're still infected. The vocal virus, something that was passed to you in the first of Sid's readings." He looked around at the pristine carpeting, looking for anything. What could he use? He looked at her handbag. "Do you have, like, tissues or something?"

She shook her head. "I can barely fit my room keys in this thing."

"You need something to stuff in your ears." Then he realized what he could use. He reached down and took off his dress shoes, ripping out the laces as he spoke. "Here."

He knotted one lace, holding it up to check the size. He knotted it again. "Look, I know it seems weird, but you've got to trust me: You need to stick this in your ear."

She took it, eyeing him. "And here I thought you were going to tie my hands again."

"This one, too," he said, handing her the second knotted string. "For the other one."

"Alex, don't be ridiculous."

"Trust me," he said.

Minhi shook her head and pulled back her hair, stuffing the knots in her eardrums. She drew the strings back so they disappeared behind her hair. "Okay?" she shouted.

"I think it'll do in a pinch," he said.

"What?"

Alex gestured. "This way."

A scream lit up from the ballroom and he looked back at her with alarm. They reached the ballroom and saw bedlam.

Alex and Minhi ran onto the floor and found people

looking about in shock. A voice was speaking over the intercom, whispering, "This is the moment of your freedom."

In the rear of the room, a group of students and adults were beating on a pair of double doors that led to another dining hall. Alex didn't see any of the debutantes, but he had a good idea where they had all gone.

Paul and Sid forced their way through the crowd. "Alex!" Paul shouted.

"Minhi, you're here," Paul said, showing visible relief. She didn't hear him but nodded.

"She's got her ears stuffed up," Alex explained.

"What, why?" Paul asked.

"Because of *that*," Alex said, pointing to the air and the droning, strange message. "What's happening?"

Paul looked unnerved, which was unusual for him. "The music cut out and all of a sudden the girls pulled their Montblancs on their parents."

"All of them?" Alex looked around.

Sid said, "All of the ones that got the pens. Well, not Minhi. So that means eleven of them."

"Is Vienna one?"

Paul shook his head. "She and her father disappeared. She looked panicked, not robotic. But forget that for now: The rest of the girls moved like vampires, Alex; they grabbed their parents and dragged them back there." He looked at Alex's socks. "How did you get here?"

"WaveRunner," Alex said, glancing up at the droning sound. "That voice is live. He's *here.* Paul—grab an ax or a fire extinguisher or something and batter those doors down. Get those people out. Sid? We've got to find him and shut him down."

Alex ran for the bar, Sid and Minhi following. A youngish bartender was on the phone trying to call for help.

"Hey!" Alex called. "Where's the intercom?"

"The bridge," the bartender said.

"Okay," Alex said to Sid and Minhi, sure that Minhi could see his lips. "Wait," he said, and ran for the orchestra, which was deserted, all the musicians having fled with the remaining parents. He emerged again with two drumsticks, their heads broken off to make them sharper, and a violin.

Sid said, "What, you're hoping to subdue him with 'The Devil Went Down to Georgia'?"

"I hate these things," Alex said, bashing the violin on the bar, and handed Sid and Minhi the drumsticks. He brandished the jagged, splintered neck of the violin, its strings hanging from the tuning bolts.

As Paul began battering away at the blocked doors

to try to rescue the parents from a horde of hypnotized girls, Alex, Sid, and Minhi hit the stairs.

The bridge was a large room at the prow of a ship on the second-to-topmost deck. Alex held up a hand again, stopping Sid and Minhi as they reached the metal door at the top of the stairs. A static charge had hit his brain. Alex put his hand on the door, waiting.

Calm down. Chill. In the past he had gotten static from a quarter mile away, but the Merrills in the van had completely caught him off guard. Just like how he had failed to listen to the static on the night of the worm, because he had been upset and distracted. Several times he had been too worked up then to listen to his own mind.

Alex was determined to master the static. He had to clear out the noise.

Alex listened, cutting through the droning of Ultravox, which wasn't for him this time. *Hear the static. Where is it?* He felt himself pointing for Sid's and Minhi's benefit.

Ultravox had lied; he might not have an army but he'd brought protection. There was too much static for it to be just one vampire. *Listen. This is what you were born to do. Pick them out.*

One on the left. One on the right. One in the center,

farther back, and powerful. He turned and said to Minhi, "You go right; I'll go left." To Sid, "You go for the microphone."

One, two, why then, 'tis time to do it.

Alex turned the doorknob and stepped back, kicking the door, causing it to fly open.

Inside, the PA echoed a half second later than Ultravox, who was speaking live in the room. Alex saw the captain and one crewman, unconscious on the floor. He turned left as a guard vampire lunged for him, and Alex dropped, letting the guard slash over him. Alex rose and swept his leg, knocking the vampire off balance, and dived, driving the violin neck into the creature's chest. Silver-and-wooden shafts from the Polibow were prime weapons, but in a pinch like this, any wood would suffice. He put all his weight on it and felt a crunch, and the vampire burst into flame.

Alex turned and looked behind him as Minhi kicked up, catching the other guard in the chin. She avoided his lunge expertly as though he were moving in slow motion. As she drove the drumstick home, she shouted, "What? I can't hear you!"

Ultravox was at a control panel, watching a closed-circuit security feed. On the black-and-white screen, Alex could see the parents, the influential, targeted ministers, pleading with their daughters, who held them all at bay and had traded their Montblancs for flashing steak knives. They had not yet delivered the killing stroke, although Ultravox seemed to be working them up into a lather. Killing someone, especially a parent, would go against every instinct, so he had to build a symphony of emotion to mask over that, to go beyond merely threatening to actually delivering the final act, the killing blow.

On the security monitor, Alex saw a large figure go into the room carrying a huge amplifier. It was Paul. He lunged for one of the debutantes and she turned around, slashing at him.

"Yes, the terror they feel is the terror you can overcome, but don't wait. Now is the time," said Ultravox, showing his fangs. He had to keep talking for the spell to work.

Alex cleared his throat as the sound from the PA cut off, ceasing the echo. The vampire snarled as he saw Sid holding an unplugged microphone cord.

"You think you know everybody," Alex said.

Ultravox swatted Sid aside and grabbed the cord, searching for an outlet.

"But you don't," Alex continued. "It's a fake. You tell people things that hurt them because you know they'll believe you."

"Alex," Ultravox said, as he turned to face him. Time slowed for a second as the vampire's eyes burrowed into his. "You're going to do something—"

"I don't think so," said Alex as he swept the violin handle, catching the vampire in the throat.

"Killthrrrmm," Ultravox gurgled, and Alex plunged the violin neck home.

A burst of brilliant flame filled the bridge as they jumped clear.

For a moment, smoke and ash rained in the small metal room and they all stood in silence. Sid finally brushed a handful of ashes out of his hair and said, "Yeah, that and his book was overrated."

Chapter 34

"So let me get this straight," Alex said as he placed a few books on the shelf of the little three-man room in New Aubrey House.

"That's the vampire shelf," Sid said, and Alex realized that the books Sid had picked up over the past weeks on his favorite subject were indeed taking up half the space. *The Vampire Encyclopedia* made an appearance, and something called *Our Vampires, Ourselves.* Alex nodded and took his own books, textbooks all, and placed them on the next shelf down.

"Get what straight?" Sangster answered. The instructor was leaning in the doorway, his hands in his pockets. He had a pair of Ray-Ban sunglasses on, as though he needed them inside.

Paul was lying on his bed across from Sid's and Alex's bunks, flipping through one of Sid's magazines. He restated Alex's question. "They *committed* them?"

"*Committed* is a strong word," Sangster replied.

"But that's it," Alex insisted, turning back. He ran his fingers along the window that looked out into the trees. "The story is the girls went crazy."

"We had ten debutantes who all tried to ice their very highly placed parents at a public gathering," Sangster said.

Paul indicated his shoulder, where his T-shirt had been pulled up to accommodate a large white bandage. "One of them took a chunk out of me, too."

"Yes, you're grievously wounded," Alex said.

"I should get time off for that," Paul muttered.

Sangster continued, "It's kind of a big deal; made Page Six back home."

"I'm sure," Alex said.

"The story will be that they got swept up in a cult. They'll all be under observation for a while. That should be the end of it."

"That's *terrible*," Alex said, frowning. "They were victims."

"Yeah." Sangster nodded quietly. "But honestly?

Thanks to you they're alive, and so are their parents. If we have to come up with a story to cover the sensational stuff, it's still better than explaining the assassination of ten ministers from ten different countries. Every meeting those ministers attend in Geneva will be heavily secured, and yet their own children provided an opportunity to get to them. I'd expect to see copycats. We're lucky they failed. Anyway, it won't be so bad. The young women will spend some time in the Alps, and in six months it will all be forgotten."

"So Ultravox knew that the meeting was coming up here in Geneva," Sid said, "and the ball for the young people was—what would you call it?—the softest target. They even threw in an attack on your researcher, Professor Montrose, to throw you off." Sid took his vampire encyclopedia off the shelf. He sat on his bunk and let it thud beside him. "You know what I think? I think you guys need to stop thinking things are over so soon."

"Yeah, that's inexcusable," Sangster said. "We were so obsessed with our database that we thought the enemy was watching the same thing. But these ten ministers were all working on Info Treaty—they were advocating a new policy for sharing electronic biographical data, to help fight human smuggling. Modernizing birth certificates, death certificates, that sort of thing."

"What does that have to do with vampires?" Alex said.

"What, you never saw *Highlander*?" Sid said. "Someone lives a long time, they can use a stolen birth certificate to reset their birth date."

Sangster nodded. "Records like that are useful to the Scholomance. So modernizing them would make their normal operations tougher. This assassination would have struck fear in the hearts of men, plus it would have been more effective than lobbying."

"Go back," Alex said, waving his hand. "You said ten."

"Sorry?"

"Ten debutantes, but there were twelve—Minhi was spared, so that leaves eleven that should have been shipped off to cult rehab." Alex looked at the teacher, trying to search the eyes behind the sunglasses. "Vienna."

"What about Vienna?" asked Minhi, who came alongside Sangster just then. She was carrying a backpack and had her hair pulled back under a cap. The weather had turned chilly and she was wearing a puffy coat.

"We're taking care of Vienna," Sangster said. "The moment she saw the other debutantes start responding to Ultravox's messages, she ran with her father and locked him in a stateroom. Then she got as far from him as possible. She was afraid she might not be spared the vampire's voice curse and she'd wind up stabbing him."

"The Scholomance has been really rough on her," Alex said, feeling helpless. "They used her brother's injuries to get her to betray her fellow students, and permanently changed her with that scarf. I'm not surprised she was afraid the worst would happen."

Sangster agreed. "Well, she waited at the stern and handed herself over to the Polidorium at her first opportunity, and we're trying to get some other help for her."

Alex understood. They—the Polidorium, with Montrose—were helping Vienna with the scarf.

Minhi nodded, looking down. "Her stuff is still in her room," she said. "I was wondering where she was."

"Anyway, this place is looking great," Sangster said. "Now that it's livable maybe we can start working on the real Glenarvon."

Alex's heart sank at the thought. He kind of liked "Glenarvon-LaLaurie."

"Don't look so crushed," Sangster said. "Otranto said months, but I'll be surprised if it's this year."

Sid cleared his throat and said, "Mr. Sangster, I hate to cut this short, but I have to go work." He had a yellow pad and a bunch of pens. He looked miserable.

"Pumpkin Show?" Sangster said, looking at his watch. "So tonight is the last one."

Sid nodded, suddenly looking kind of pale. "It's the first one I'm doing without using the book."

"Who needs it? Anyway, I was just stopping by." Sangster had an apartment now, in another wing of the house. Alex had heard it was about the size of three of these student rooms. "You guys have made good guests," Sangster said. "Very good guests." And with that he was gone.

Chapter 35

Sid's story that night was called "After the Transfer."

As Sid approached the chair, Alex knew that "After the Transfer" would be a disaster. Sid had lost his nerve since leaving the library. He had hunkered down in a bay window in New Aubrey House with a legal pad and pen, and started strong: Alex checked in on him and saw outlines taped to the window, and even outlines of how Sid was going to use the next few hours ("2:00–3:00 BRAINSTORM. 3:00–4:00 OUTLINE. 4:00–4:45 WRITE. 4:45–5:30 REVISE."). Alex stopped in again around five, and Sid was sitting and scrawling amid piles of yellow wads of paper. He had no idea if Sid was in revise mode or not. The boy looked panicked.

And now Sid trudged toward the big chair with feet dragging, his arms swaying as though his hands were dull wads of meat, the papers weighing him down.

Sid sat under the candles and the room hushed. Alex heard the creak of wooden seats as students leaned forward. The yodeler girl, Ilsa, was not among them; a debutante with a highly placed parent, Ilsa was among those now recuperating in the Alps.

"'After the Transfer,'" Sid read.

He was silent, then, for what seemed like a minute and a half.

Finally the tension broke, and Sid opened his mouth. Alex looked in his friend's eyes and saw something like desperate panic. Sid's hands shook, but when he spoke, he sounded still.

"It has been twenty-three years since I have spoken of our time in the garden," read Sid, "and after tonight I shall not speak of it again."

And off into the far reaches of story went Sid, and Alex realized he had been duped by his own eyes.

And also proven right after all: Sid did not need the spell in the book, for he had spells of his own.